LIGHTNING BUTTERFLIES

CATCHING THE TELEPORTATION BUG

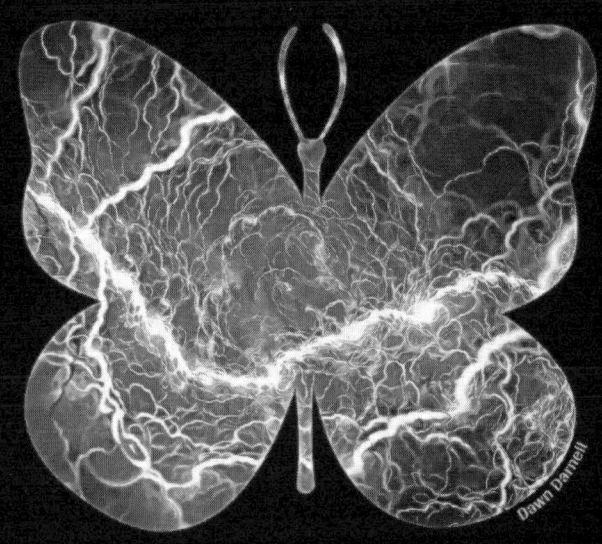

REV. JIM H. DARNELL, JR.

Copyright © 2022 by James Hugh Darnell Jr.

All rights reserved. No parts of this book may be reproduced in any form or by electronic or mechanical means, including information storage and retrieval systems, without permission in writing from the publisher, except by reviewers, who may quote brief passages in a review.

Cataloging in Publication Data

Lightning Butterflies: Catching the Teleportation Bug

ISBN: 979-8844075896

Independently published in

August 2022

Cover design: Dawn Darnell

Other books by Jim H. Darnell Jr.
    Because of you, I Lost Everything!
    A Cause de Toi, J'ai Tout Perdu!

TABLE OF CONTENTS

Chapter 1 – The Screeching Halt.....**5**

Chapter 2 – The Hotdog Stand.....**13**

Chapter 3 – Amy.....**19**

Chapter 4 – Sunset.....**29**

Chapter 5 – The Adventure Begins.....**41**

Chapter 6 – Teleportation.....**47**

Chapter 7 – The Mask.....**55**

Chapter 8 – The Babies and the Hippo.....**61**

Chapter 9 – The Rock and the Green Mamba.....**67**

Chapter 10 – Christianity Origen.....**71**

Chapter 11 – Found.....**81**

Chapter 12 – Lost Love.....**85**

Chapter 13 – Fruit Bats.....**89**

Chapter 14 – Conditioner.....**95**

Chapter 15 – The Out-of-Control Experiment.....**99**

Chapter 16 – Caught.....**107**

Chapter 17 – On the Run.....**115**

Chapter 18 – Shoot'em Up.....**121**

Chapter 19 – Fugitives.....**129**

Chapter 20 – Kidnapped.....**135**

Chapter 21 – Mastering Teleportation.....**139**

Chapter 22 – The Robberies.....**147**

Chapter 23 – The Butterfly Wing.....**151**

Chapter 24 – The Park....**159**

Chapter 25 – The Plan?.....**171**

Chapter 26 – Monkabe.....**175**

CHAPTER 1
THE SCREECHING HALT

"Stop! Stop right now!" screamed Mickey. "Stooop!" Mickey then added an involuntary throw-up response as he heaved with his mouth closed, "Bleaahhug!"

"Why?" responded the bus driver who was trying to maintain control over the situation.

The two ladies in front of Mickey hysterically screamed, "Stop! Let him out of here! STOP! Let him out of here!" Mickey was in the very back. He was pinched between the side of the van and a mountain of bags to his left. They had been riding in the van all day. The roads were very nice in spots where they could drive at highway speeds but then hit spots in the roads that were washed out from the rains. The driver would slow down with all urgency, but they would still slam into the potholes. For the two sitting up front, hitting dirt was an inconvenience. To Mickey all the way in the back, it was a pounding. Over and over again, he was thrown upwards where he would hit the ceiling had it not been for his seatbelt. The seatbelt violently worked and slammed him downs hard as the potholes slung him upwards. As quickly as he came back down again, the road bounced him back up again. Mickey could not use his hands to brace himself for he had other problems as well. He felt like he was in quicksand being sucked down and would disappear if the luggage toppled on top of him. Mickey bravely fought with his hands to avoid being buried by the suitcases. The bouncing from the road and the seatbelt aggressively slamming Mickey around, yet not going anywhere, had the luggage ramming Mickey into the side of the vehicle.

Mickey was the one really suffering, but it was the two ladies who were squealing like pigs, "Let him out of here!" Before the vehicle came to a complete stop, Mickey vaulted over the middle seat. He would have taken the aisle, but it was filled with large suitcases as well. He drove a knee into the first lady's shoulder. Almost instantaneously, he threw a foot into the second lady's neck.

In the front passenger seat sat a gray-haired man, named Red. As the van was lurching to a stop, he unbuckled, opened his door, and hopped out at the same moment. He opened the sliding van door and gave it a shove. Mickey jumped out like he was a frog. His knees were locked in by his chest and he jumped. Before he could land, he projected another "Bleaahhug!", but this time his mouth was wide open. He landed feet spread apart. Again, he screamed, "Bleaahhug!" "Bleaahhug!" "Bleaahhug!" After the fourth one, nothing else came out, but he screamed, "Bleaahhug!" "Bleaahhug!" "Bleaahhug!" Mickey felt like his body was being ripped apart for it was fighting the violent treatment as hard as it could through involuntary convulsions.

His mother was driving. Sabrina ran around to help her son, but she did not know what to do. She was waving her hands frantically trying to figure out a solution. Red rushed in between his mother and Mickey. He grabbed Mickey around the waist with both arms and squeezed the stomach hard. To Mickey's surprise, the strong arms pinched the fight out of his body. After a few moments, Red sat Mickey down cautiously. Just like Red had slid in between Mickey and his mother, she now glided in and hugged Mickey from behind.

Mickey's aunt and grandmother quickly demonstrated love and paranoia at the same time. They opened their purses, and removed and donned masks. They reached into their purses again to grab latex gloves. With simple efficient motion, they slid their hands into the gloves. Their motions were synchronized in a way that only a mother and daughter could. For a third time, they plunged into their purses, this time they removed alcohol wipes. After ripping the wrapper, they began to clean up Mickey. As if in a chorus, where separating one voice from another is nearly impossible, the two ladies spoke, "Oh poor thing!" "How terrible!" "You must feel awful!" "You lost everything you ate!" "That must really hurt!" They grabbed his hands and started cleaning. As if sprung to action by a bell, immediately and in unison, the two opened their purses again. They pulled out another wipe, ripped it open, and started working on Mickey's face.

Mickey fought back and pushed their hands away, but the two ladies ignored his protests and immediately started washing his face again. Mickey exclaimed, "I was careful! I made sure that I did not throw up on myself. I did not get any on my hands or my face." His relatives driven by fear, spoke "Yes!" "Impressive, but there are still germs!" "You can't be too careful!"

Mickey chose to end the scene, "I am not contagious. I don't have an illness! I don't have bad germs! I just sat in the back seat too long."

Red opened the front door and decided to rescue Mickey. He reached down to pick up Mickey, his mother was still holding him from behind. She let go. He snagged the lad; and in a big swoop, he set the child in the front seat. He then proceeded to the back where Mickey sat.

Insignificant to the moment, yet central to the story, a blue car rushed past them kicking up dust. The dust spewed up in the air and poisoned the air orange. Mother and daughter with their masks on were coughing up a storm. The others breathing the same air without masks just stared at the two. The boy looked up at Red and said, "Now you have met my aunt and grandmother."

When the two ladies realized that they were the only ones seemingly affected by the air, they defended themselves, "We have really sensitive lungs." "Really sensitive!" "If you had our lungs, you would understand!"

The only man there found his new, self-appointed seat in the back. It was a really tight fit for an adult man, he pondered, "Is this what I had come halfway across the world to experience?"

A few minutes later, Sabrina exclaimed, "We are here in an area of legendary faith. A land where their faith beats so hard that they had chosen to risk everything for God!" Red knew he needed to see such faith himself! He looked around, the people were rich enough to have nice clothes, and have eaten enough to be fitly built. Most walked. Few had bikes or motorcycles. The streets lacked cars. The houses were little shacks. The difference between the rich and poor was that some houses had tin roofs and others had thatched roofs made of sticks and straw. Red thought to himself, "Here in this forgotten land, I have chosen to find answers to life!"

The blue car that had kicked up the dust, was slowly driving through the village. Gus screamed out, "Ma, are you sure you have this all figured out?" "This is the place all right." "I am not talking about the place. The sun is going to set soon, where are we going to spend the night?" "Relax!" "That is the point, Ma! How can we relax when I am hungry and we have nothing to eat?" "You worry too much! Soon you will be able to buy anything you want for the rest of your life." "But I have been hungry all day." "Shut up!" replies his brother. "You think you always know what is best, Gene!" "That is not my name." "Well Gene … ius, you know everything, but how to plan a simple meal!" "Shut up!" "No, you shut up!" Ma yells, "You are acting like children!" In unison, the boys yell, "We are your children!"

> "You call me a genius. Let me tell you a few stories. This land is full of tales of people being turned into wild beasts

at night. Some because they practice witchcraft. Others because they were cursed by those who practice witchcraft. If their friends and family found out that one of their loved ones would turn into a wild animal at night, they would kill that person. At night, the one who would transform into a beast would find refuge in the jungle where no one could find out the secret. Even that is far from safe because the night must be spent hiding in the jungle hoping not to be shot by a hunter. The one who becomes a wild animal can't tell a soul of the spell for everyone would be afraid - such a lonely life. Someone who chose to become a wild animal always became the most ferocious animal. That is why a spirit person can predict that a wild beast is going to kill someone."

"Those are just superstitions. They are legends passed on by some to maintain power." Gus answers in almost a whisper.

"Are you sure? You may call these superstitions, but even the most level-headed Africans have stories. Stories about people they know. Stories of hunters who spotted antelope. They were patient until they had the right shot. They pulled the trigger and watched the animal fall. They walked over to their prize, only to find their friend lying dead. Even the police understand the power of witchcraft, and they don't consider shooting someone who had transformed into a wild animal a crime."

"You are just messing with me!" "Am I? What about the stories of medicine men saying to someone they wish to curse and proclaim, 'You will be eaten by a lion!' Sure enough, not long after that, the family witnessed a lion attack their loved one."

"You're just trying to scare me." "You're right, I am trying to scare you, but with real stories. Just go ask the Africans." "Mom, tell him to quit!" "Gene stop torturing your brother." Gene pushed a little bit more. "It is the legends that brought us to

Africa. We are here to chase down a power." All of a sudden, Gene lunges at his brother and yells, "Aaauuh!" Startled, Gus jumped back and rammed into the side of the car. A loud "thunk" reverberated in the car as a head met the window. Gene and their mother spewed out in laughter. Both mother and son yelled, "Gus!" "My name is not Gus!" "You jumped like a Gussst of air grabbed you. Wait! Except there is no wind in this car!" Mother was adamant, "You have always jumped like a gust of wind." An obvious lie became the defense. "I did not jump; I had a cramp." Gene, "You always have cramps when I scare you!" Ma, "Your brother does make a good point."

Gene changed the subject, "There can be profit in turning people into animals, but there is another fable that is really profitable." "What is that Genius?" "Gust!" "Genius!" "Gust!" Ma blurts, "Just tell him now that we are here, and he can't run back home to his mommy. Oh, wait," The two instigators chime in unison, "Mommy is not home!" They jumped into a dance the best they could in the car. Hands in the air rocked back and forth and their bodies squirmed like a worm. In unison, they sang, "Mommy's not home! Mommy's not home!" They finished with a huge belly laugh with their hands over their stomach and they just rolled in their seats." Gus replied, "Genius, just watch the road! You are going to get us all killed!" Gene mocked, "I think we just struck a nerve!" In a remorseful voice, Ma said, "Ahh!" For three seconds, the car was completely silent, then they belly laughed one more time, except with much greater exaggeration. They laughed louder and slid down to the floorboard. Gus struck back, "You can count on this Ma. I would never run to you for comfort." Ma replied in a series of many notes, "Aahhooh! You don't appreciate all that your mother has done for you – an ungrateful child!"

Red walked around the open market. Everyone had their wares out. Tomatoes were piled in groups of five. There was fruit galore. The avocados were so big, that they appeared to have come from a fantasy world. The bellies of the green bubbles were the size of a grapefruit. Red wondered - did such giant avocados taste the same as the little ones he found back home? Red recognized the leafy tops of the pineapples. The pineapples were knee-high and were like nothing he had seen before. Everything seemed weird and out of place. Red understood nothing spoken. The tribal tongue was totally incomprehensible.

Red heard commotion off to his left. He looked up to see the Africans had gathered around mother and daughter. A lot of the Africans said, "Hunh!" In astonishment as the two ladies pulled out in harmony a glove to put on. They worked it on one hand. They reached in their bag and pull out a second glove and worked it over the other hand. Once again, in reaction to the perfect action symphony, the locals echoed, "Hunh!" The Africans by then sprawled into a huge crowd that enveloped the two. Red could barely see them; he moved a little. Red was fascinated by the puzzlement of the Africans. He knew this next one would really get a reaction. As the crowds increased, the ladies became flustered because they were not ready for all the germy contaminants radiating from the crowd. They quickly reached in one more time, this time for face masks. They placed the band behind the head, and in a swift motion, they pulled the mask over the face and anchored the white shield over the mouth and nose.

An African came really close to Red and pivoted until he was six inches away. Red's heartbeat was hard, "What is this man going to do to me?" For once, English was heard, "Are they sick?" Red simply answered, "No!" "Hunh!" The man was just stunned and just did not know what to say next. Red spoke again, "No, they are not sick!" "Hunh!"

CHAPTER 2
THE HOTDOG STAND

"Hotdogs! Hotdogs!" came the voice from the other side of the market. Red started making his way over. Red discovered that there was no direct route to the merchant. Merchant stands were everywhere. People were very courteous and moved so that he could get by. After a few seconds, all the familiar surroundings were gone. He had entered into a sea of black. The lone bleached one was definitely out of place, but he was offered respect, as people tried to let him by. "Hotdogs! Hotdogs!" Red wondered why he was even making his way over to the stand for he ate hotdogs, but he was definitely not overly fond of them either. Yet something about the familiar was drawing him for the voice was so soothing to his ears. "Hotdogs! Hotdogs! Come and get them while they last." Red had no clue that this assuring voice was calling him down a most terrifying path.

Gene gloated, "See, I am taking care of you. I always have!" Ma joined in, "My poor darling, you always feel so mistreated." They were driving up an alley that had never been maintained. One side of the road was so polluted with trash that even the grass wouldn't grow and it was completely slimed over in plastic bags. The bags were covered by another layer of trash – water bottles, cans, and some fresh produce peelings. On the far side of the layer of trash that covered the road edge was a receding grass line as the trash grew with each passing day. The left wheels of the car hugged the trash line because the drainage crater between the two tracks had nearly made that road impassable.

The road was on a slight incline giving the feeling that if the wheels would roll over the trash, the car would just slide down into the thick underbrush.

They pulled up to a hotel. The gate was locked. Gene just honked his horn and waited. Before long, a heavy clacking sound was heard as someone was fumbling to open the gate. A long high pitched, "Unnnrrrr!" squealed as metal rubbed on metal. As soon as it stopped, the metal gates started to swing inwards. Another grinding metal sound echoed as the hinges toted the doors out of the way. Gene stated, "You never believe us, but we always take care of you." "Always!" Resounded Ma. "After all these years, you still doubt us!" They both shook their heads.

Red stopped a couple of yards away from the hotdog cart. It was a standard hotdog cart, but the hand-painted food wagon seemed to be trying to tell a story. The sky was black and dark on the cart – it gave the feeling that a most terrible storm was about to hit. Everywhere were lightning bolts. Faces were bodiless. What made the faces eerie was that they were not connected to anything. The final object on the cart was some strange butterfly. The butterfly wings were the blackest black, with yellow dots lined in descending order. The yellow streaks on the wings appeared to be lightning bolts. The butterflies like the rest of the cart told of lightning in the darkest of nights.

Ma yelled, "Hurry up! I want to go out to the fields where the magic happens." Gene spoke to his brother, "You need to see these fields where the most incredible power is unleashed." Gus answered hesitantly, "What fields? What magical power?" "Faces appeared and disappeared in the crackling of lightning. According to the stories, you could be looking across a field darkened by the heaviness of impending rain. When the lightning struck, it carried faces. The loudest thunder you ever did hear shook the air. The hairs on the arms stood up from the electrical charge. All around was such incredible power. Just like that …" Gene snapped his fingers with one hand and thudded the other hard into Gus's chest. Gus jumped backward. With a sure grip, Gene yanked Gus with all his might until the two were so close yet their faces did not touch. "Just like that!" Gene started again, "A face that was nowhere to be seen is now within licking touch distance."

Red spoke out to the hotdog salesman, "All the hotdog wagons I have ever seen are cheery colored to attract customers. Yours is storm covered with faces, butterflies, and lightning." Monkabe spoke out! "Ha yes! You are correct about the other carts, but Monkabe's cart tells a story." Monkabe pulled a plump hotdog out of boiling water with his tongs and placed it on a bun. He opened the condiment tray and scooped up some greenish goo with little red squares in it, and spread it across the top of the hotdog. Monkabe handed it to Red.

Immediately, he took a bite out of the hotdog, and declared, "This is good! What about the lightning and stuff?" "There is a legend around here that in thunderstorms, people appear and disappear." "We call that a campfire story." Monkabe looked puzzled, "A campfire story!" "Yes, people gather around campfires. We can all imagine the monsters beyond the light and into the shadows. We tell stories of impossible tales that somehow seem so believable. We try to outspook each other. At the end of the night, even the smallest sound is made by the scariest monsters. We wonder if we will sleep at all – that is campfire stories!" "Ah, yes! This African land is full of power. You find the kind of power you look for!" Red said, "I did not come to Africa to see people appear and disappear in my face!" "You did come to find answers." Red continued, "Answers to daily problems, not to chase superstitions." Monkabe reached under the cart as he continued to talk. "You see this butterfly? They are now out in the fields. Go catch some." "But that is not what I came here for!" "Go catch some butterflies! Start the adventure. What else are you going to do this afternoon?" Monkabe continued "The kind of answers you look for cannot be found. Live and discover answers, besides nothing else is going on!" Monkabe handed Red two nets and a cage. "Two nets?" "Yes, two!" "But …" Red's head fell. Monkabe continued with great confidence, "Your old life is forever broken, a new adventure awaits. Two!"

The clients donning gloves confused everyone. Someone came up to them and spoke to them, "Are you doctors?" "No." Came the reply. Many voices echoed, "Hunh?" Before the two ladies took a drink, they each removed a small packet from their purses and tore open the alcohol wipes. They removed the wipes in unison and proceeded to open their bottles. They wiped off the top that had been sealed anyway, and spoke, "You can't be too careful." "No, you can't!"

Mickey and his mom found a souvenir table with some really wide and flat figurines of girls. The head was six inches wide, but only half an inch thick. As soon as she picked one up for her son, the whole place became extremely crowded. His mom asked, "Wouldn't you like one to take back home? It is, after all, the first souvenir we have found." The protest came, "But it is of a girl!" Mickey had one in his hands while he was staring at it intently. He spun it all around from side to top of head to bottom of feet trying to figure out why the doll was extra wide and super thin. Mom asked, "What is the doll for? Why is it so skinny and wide?" The saleswoman spoke to an interpreter, "The doll goes on the back like this!"

The lady bent over forward enough so that she could lay the doll in the middle of her back and for the doll not to have fallen off. Mickey was holding his figurine fairly close to his chest as he stopped and watched. The lady grabbed a huge cloth and wrapped herself snuggly which tied the doll on the back. She stood upright and the body of the figurine was wedged tightly against the woman by the cloth. Only the figurine's head could be seen above the cloth.

The vendor stated, "People walk around all day with the doll on the back." Mickey's mom asked, "Why do people do that?" The response was simple, "The doll is carried on the back like a baby – like that woman!" She pointed to a lady who was carrying a baby on the back. Just like the doll, a large cloth firmly held the baby on the back with only the head that could be seen above the wrap. The whole crowd was waiting in eager anticipation for the saleswoman to complete her explanation. The sales lady fully explains, "It is a prayer to the spirits to become pregnant!"

Mickey who was holding a doll closely quickly threw the doll down on the ground. He immediately coughed with hysterical agitation. He ran off, bent over from coughing with one hand way out in front as if that hand would have dug a hole through the crowd, and created an escape from the horrifying humiliation. People moved out of the way to let the greatly embarrassed kid pass. Many mimicked the situation. Some were bent over and coughing with a hand out in front while others laughed at them. Others were placing a pretend doll on the back. They wrapped themselves in an invisible cloth. They dropped to their knees and with fingers folded in a praying manner. As if that was not enough, the hands immediately reached up to heaven with the head staring as if unto God.

The woman spoke one last time, "I don't think he is going to pray today to become pregnant." A couple of the young men around walked bowed backward with their hands resting on an enormous invisible belly. The laughter filled the market.

CHAPTER 3
AMY

Back in the United States, the mood was not nearly so jolly. A young lady yanked with all her might on a lawnmower cord. She heard a fading and slowing, "Da, da, da, da!" She yanked again, "Da, da, da, da, da!" She heaved again, "Da, da, da, da, da!" She wiped her forehead with her forearm. Once again, she pulled, "Da, da, da, da, da!" She yelled out loud, "I will not!" She tugged again, "Da, da, da, da, da!" "Absolutely no way!" She heaved again, "Da, da, da, da, da!" She persisted, "Da, da, da, da, da!" "I got this!" She planted her feet just right. She braced herself for the biggest pull. She ripped the cord backward with all the strength she could muster, but it was like she was in slow motion. This time the sputtering engine was, "Da, da, da!" Her strength was gone. Amy left the lawnmower in the yard and walked into the house, "No, no, no, no, no!" Amy huddled in her car and drove off.

Ma and her two sons were standing in the middle of a field. Gus smarted off, "Why are we standing here? Are we waiting for it to rain? There is not even a breeze." Gus then mocked them for his nickname. "There is not even a GGUUUSSS … t of wind here. Storms always follow gusts of wind." Ma ripped back, "We are trying to make you rich and provide for you. All you can do is mock us!" "Mock you? No, no, no, no, no! I would never mock you. I am just wondering how long we are going to stand in the middle of this field." The three of them just continue to stare into the open space of the field.

Red walked to the edge of the village with two nets on poles and one butterfly cage. "Two? Really two? Exactly what I am to do with this second net? Two I guess it is!" Just then Mickey came running up from behind, and blurted, "Wait up!" Red looked back and saw Mickey sprinting up. "Two!" He pauses, taking a moment. He continued walking forward without looking back. He reached out holding a pole as he stared forward. "Two is just perfect!" Mickey grabbed a pole and yelled, "Thanks!" Red asked, "What is the rush?" "Nothing, I was just wanting to get away!" "Get away from what?" Mickey did not answer. "Look, you might as well tell me. I will hear all about it. You would rather me hear your side first." "Mom tried to give a fertility doll." "We came here for miracles, but that would be a really bad miracle." Mickey started the bent-over-backward pregnant waddle, "Me being like this is just gross."

Red changed the subject, "How about going butterfly hunting with me?" "That sounds perfect!" "We are not looking for just any butterfly. We are looking for the darkest black butterfly with lightning flashes and lightbulbs on it." "Sounds like an awesome butterfly." "It is just like the one painted on the hotdog stand with a man yelling 'Hotdogs!'" "I did not see any stand or hear anyone yelling, 'Hotdogs!' Believe me, I would have gone there, I love hotdogs!" Red became serious, "You did not see a stand? It was the tallest thing in the market. You could not have missed it!" Mickey stopped and stared at Red, "You are just telling me stories." Red argued back, "No, absolutely not, the hotdog stand was so obvious. You are just telling me stories."

Gene calls out, "Come look at this! Here are ants like nothing we have ever seen before." Ma and Gus came over and stared at the little critters. Ma, "Notice that army ants possess hardened bodies like a beetle and shed their shells." Gene contributes, "The soldier army ants so gallantly collected all husks and have made a tunnel for the worker ants." Gus declares, "The soldier army ants are the most chivalrous in all the animal kingdom." Ma continues the thought, "Look, every inch or so, one of the soldier ants guards facing outwards to protect the smaller females. Huddled together, the worker ants are forming an endless line racing under the shell canopy. Unlike other animals, where the bulls attack one another for dominance, like you two, these courteous soldier ants in unison protect all the worker ants."

Gene continued, "Look how chivalrous the male ants are. They are standing guard and they have built a tunnel for the females. How romantic?" Gus joked as well, "I have never seen such gallantry in my life. How inspiring!" Gene poked, "Ma, why didn't you teach us to be such gentlemen as these ants are." Ma responded, "I sure tried, but you two never listened. My life would be so much better if I was treated like the lady I am."

Gene was stupefied, "I have never, ever, seen such honor, respect and such gentlemen in all my life." Gus was amazed, "These are the most honorable males I have ever seen." Ma smarted off, "I guess that proves it, females are just superior to males." Gene argues, "No, Ma, the smaller females are doing nothing great. They are just running in safety; it's the male soldier ants risking their lives standing guard." Ma replied gloatingly, "Don't you know anything about ants? All the ants are females. The worker ants are females. The soldier ants are females. They only keep a few men around for the necessity of reproduction." Gene prodded, "Are you trying to tell me that these soldier ants with the horns are females?" "Ma boasted, "I sure am! These most chivalrous ants are females. These very best of the best of what a man is supposed to be are females. That proves it. Females are better than even the best of men."

Gus replied, "They may act with great honor, but I wonder how vicious they are?" Gene continues, "I imagine army ants are the most vicious of all. Look at the soldier ants, they all have horns." Gene picked up a stick and placed the tip right in front of a soldier ant. The ant bowed back even more in so raising the horns above the head. The ant just stood there. Gene pushed the stick forward until the army ant crawled upon it. He slung the branch upwards until the ant was right in front of Gus. "Take it, and see if it is ferocious." Gus stood there paralyzed.

Gene grew impatient. "I am not waiting to see if you will find any manhood." Gene spun the stick back to himself. He cupped his free hand and scooped the ant into it. He leaned the stick against his leg. He then pinched the ant between his fingers where the head was pinned and could not attack. In following, he set a finger directly in front of the horns. The ant planted his head in Gene's finger. He snapped shut the horns. Gene raised his finger for all to view the ant embedded in and dangling, "See, nothing to it! Are you ready yet to be a man?" With the stick, Gene raised another soldier ant. With one quick motion, the ant was parked right in front of Gus' face.

Gus displayed his manliness by quickly shoving his finger in the ant's face until the soldier ant latched onto his finger by sinking his horns into the flesh. Gus claimed, "The army ant is not all that tough! Their pinchers are nothing." Gene smiled, "If it is nothing, see what the worker ant will do." Gene planted the tip of the stick into the ant runway and the ants took off up the stick. Once again, the stick was placed in front of Gus. Gus snatched one ant, and immediately he was bit by the worker ant. His eyes grew big and he turned around so that no one else could see his pain. Gene could tell from Gus' muffled reaction that the bite was fierce. Still, too proud to not take his turn, Gene snagged his own ant. Immediately, he started twisting like he was doing the potty dance. Ma spoke out, "So that is manhood! Count me out!" Gus declared triumphantly, "That worker ant has much or more venom than any wasp I ever met." Gene, "That is an attention-getter! My finger is going to swell up." Gus blared, "If this viciousness is what a real lady is like, I don't want one!" "Me, neither!" chimed in Gene.

The grass had just been cut with the green blades sawed off at the base making it logically impossible for anything to hide.

With all the focus on the ants, they had missed the biggest threat. Within inches of their feet, there was a snake. The short body was about 18 inches long. The skin was splotched brown. Upon being spotted, the head reared back into attack mode. The snake attempted pathetically to back out of the situation. The snake only had the half-asleep speed gear. The mouth was fully opened displaying the two fangs. Ma yelled out, "There are only two kinds of snakes in Africa. Those that give you time for one last prayer and those who don't." Gene whispered, "This snake is so slow that prey has to fall over dead immediately for the snake to catch up to it."

Gus stated, "Look at that distinctive head, it is a puff adder." Ma asks, "Is it really deadly?" Gus responded, "Puff adders kill more people in all of Africa than all other snakes and animals combined." Gene contributed, "I would call that deadly!"

The snake turned and tried to escape the situation. Gene stepped on the snake's head. Gus removed his pocket knife and severed the head. Once detached, Gene removed his foot. Both the detached head and the body remained motionless. A brilliant idea swept over Gene, "Let's drop the snake in the ants!" Gene utilized his stick once more to lift the limp snake and the snake plummeted into the ant's pathway. The ants pounced all over the snake, stinging it ferociously. The snake folded in half, braided itself and slithered back and forth all over itself from the toxin of the ant bites.

Amy opened the door to a diner. She marched up to the counter and ordered a lemonade. She took her drink and sat down. In came some girls her age and they planted themselves in front of her table. They took turns jeering with each trying to outdo the other through dainty cruelty. "Why look it is Amy!" "So, what are your big plans now that you have graduated from high school?" Another said, "Oh, wait, sitting alone drinking lemonade is her big life's plan." "Poor Amy, even her dad can't stand her so he fled to Africa!" Amy sat there pretending to be very calm. She never looked at them nor acknowledged their presence. The highly privileged sometimes see themselves as classy, yet somehow are so low class. They spewed out another round of taunting. "She is trying to ignore us." "Just like she is trying to ignore life sitting here all alone with no future!" The third somehow found a way to outdo herself in brutality. "Take a really close look at her – I mean a really close look at her!" One girl walked around the table and lifted up Amy's hair to look at it. The other cocked her head just like a little puppy dog would do when seeing something new and strange for the first time. The nose stayed in place while the chin angled right and the crown of the head slid left. The last continued, "I mean take a really close look at her! She is exactly what I don't want to be." All three roared in laughter. Amy hopped up and stormed off. "No wonder no guy will date her!" "A temper like that is really frightening!" "What a loser!"

Ma, Gene, and Gus were standing exactly where they were a while ago staring across an empty field. From the right, Red and Mickey appeared. They were each chasing butterflies. Mickey was swinging wildly, and the butterfly kept bouncing out of the net's grasp. Red moved all slow and caught his butterfly with ease. Red spun the handle 180 degrees to entrap the butterfly in the lower portion of the net. Red pulled the net in close. Mickey swung once more, then yelled, "I got him. I got him!" Mickey stopped and the butterfly flew back out of the net. Mickey yelled in a quick staccato, "Hey, hey, hey, hey!" He quickly swung back upward to keep the butterfly from escaping. "How do you keep this thing from escaping? Red emitted a gentle laugh.

Gus, Ma, and Gene were just standing there at the edge of the field watching Mickey and Red capture butterflies. Gus confessed sarcastically, "So this is why we went halfway around the world – just to watch Americans capture butterflies. We could have done this back at home!" Ma reminded him, "Their fantasy is catching butterflies; ours is stealing the world. Be patient my son."

Amy rushed back home and slammed her car door without realizing it. She looked back and tried to ease herself, "I gotta calm down. I gotta calm down, but I am not calling him. There is no way I am calling him." She rumbled over to the lawnmower. She placed one hand on the push bar and the other on the starter pull handle. She let go of the pull knob and placed both hands on the push bar. "If this does not, work nothing will!" She pushed the mower off the grass and onto the sidewalk. She began running with all her might. Once the mower reached top speed, she grabbed the nob and yanked back with all her might while still pushing with the other hand. The mower thundered – well almost thundered. It sputtered like it was going to start then faded away, "Da, da, da, da, da, da, da, da, da!" "You gotta be kidding me!" She turned the mower around and raced back down the sidewalk attempting another push start. Once again, some black smoke sputtered, but very quickly all was quiet. "I told myself, I would never call him. Dad has learned to do things without help and so can I. I don't need a man to come to my rescue. Awww!"

Amy stormed into the house and moments later she reemerged with a card in her hand. She claimed, "I can't believe this is happening to me." She dialed the number. "Hello Zach, this is Amy! … Yeah, I know Dad made arrangements for me to call you if I need anything, but I assured him that I would not be calling you. … I know he told you I would fight to call you! … The mower will not start."

The sun was setting in Africa. Red and Mickey's little cage was full of butterflies. Red admitted, "It is getting dark." Mickey continued, "And, we have a cage jam-packed with butterflies. The kind for your quest." We had better return the cage to Monkabe" added Red. Mickey looked over at the three still standing in the field, "It is weird that they are standing there watching us catch butterflies. I am sure they are trouble." "Ein, we will probably never see them again." "I hope you are right."

Almost immediately, Zach appeared and Amy was still standing over the mower. Amy blurted, "I just can't get this mower to start!" Zach did not say anything, and Amy just had a hard time not filling in the void. "Pa, got his wish!" Zach responded, "I know. He has been trying to get us to meet for a long time." "That is for sure." Zach popped the spark plug wire off the spark plug. The only thing Zach carried in his hand was a spark plug wrench. He slipped the mouth of the socket over the spark plug, then effortlessly ratcheted the spark plug off. Amy asked, "Is that the problem?" "It looks like it! You see how it is all black and burned." came the answer. With his left hand, he reached into his back pocket and pulled out some sandpaper. He quickly scraped the black off the terminals which left shiny metal.

Zach began to play his game. Although he was not sure what he thought of Amy, he was certain that she needed uplifting. "Red told me over and over again, 'She is so cute!'" Amy blushed, as her cheeks started to glow a little red. "When your pa finished telling me that you are really cute. He would start over and say, "She is really cute. I am sure you will really like her!"

By then, Zach was already screwing the spark plug back in. Amy did not expect Zach to be so blunt, but she was glad that things were out in the air. Amy knew that Zach was trying to embarrass her, so she tried her turn at embarrassing him, "So what do you think?" Zach played all innocent, "Think about what?" "What Pa said about me being cute and all." Zach's response on the outside was far more confident than his insides were. He knew that she had been really hurt, but she possessed a beauty and a charm that could have so easily melted him if he would have let it.

Zach answered the 'cute' question, "You are definitely cute. In fact, you are stunningly breathtaking." Before she had a chance to respond, Zach continued, "About the other – me liking you – that is still up for debate." Amy protected herself, "Don't get any ideas!" Zach put her back in her place. "If I had any ideas, I would not have fixed your mower in no time flat." Zach stood up and stepped between her and the push bar with his back turned to her. He gave a half-pull The yank looked effortless, but in the brief moment he pulled, he jerked as fiercely as he could to maximize the super-abbreviated tug. The engine purred for a few seconds and then he let go to turn off the engine.

He turned around and stared at her, "All you had to do is pull!" With that last zinger, he turned and walked away. Amy was not blushing just a little then; she was pretending that the glowing was red hot in anger. Mixed in with all sorts of emotions was a great wonder. In his retreat, he walked tall and squarely away from her. He did not wish for her to see the huge grin on his face. It was just a game that turned out well this time. He knew he had baited and hooked her; but at the same time, he was trying not to admit to himself that he was hooked on her.

She had never, ever had anyone gush without drooling over her looks. He made her feel like such a treasure and so unneeded both at the same time. She said nothing while he walked away, but she could not help cracking a smile behind his back.

CHAPTER 4
SUNSET

Red and Mickey arrived back at the village at sunset. All the merchants were gone including Monkabe. The next day was Sunday – the day they had come for. Normally, when Americans went overseas to visit churches, they went on mission trips where they would do activities for kids, or medicine like health or dental. Red who had been active in church all his life, did not come to serve – he came to see.

This little town had three hotels. One hotel was the nicest. From hearing the mother and her daughter, you would not believe it. The hotel clerk had a translator who explained. "We have buckets of water in your room. We will keep filling up your buckets of water as needed from the well." The mother and her daughter took turns exclaiming, "You mean this hotel has no running water?" "We got to have running water." "I have never heard of such!" "No running water!" "This is not the stone age." "You have sinks, but no water." "There is a shower that does not function!" "And worst of all – the toilet." "How can you have a toilet without water?" "You go, but you can't see it go?" "That is so absurd!" "Why do you not have water?" "Tell us!" The poor clerk tried to explain this through the interpreter, "The city has not connected water to this neighborhood."

Mother and daughter continued their outrage, "I will not have it!" "You need to take us elsewhere!" "This is totally unacceptable!" "Let's go immediately!" What they did not realize was they were insulting the clerk and his hotel. The hotel had six rooms at $20 a night. At best, the hotel could net $120 a night. The clerk receives a very modest salary. This family built what they could afford. It was not a grand hotel, but it was the family's jewel. Their best was totally unacceptable. Sabrina was trying to calm down her mother and her sister, "You two are embarrassing yourselves. You are coming across as spoiled brats." "How are we supposed to wash all the germs away if there is not even running water?" "Yeah, tell us that!" Sabrina explained, "There is nowhere to go! There are three hotels. One has running water!" The two interject, "Then let's go!" Sabrina continued a little slower, "One has running water some of the time, but its looks will gross you out and it stinks. Sabrina continued on, "Do you really want running water for a few hours every day and live where it smells like something has died?" The two chimed in, "We want the third hotel then!" "It is settled." Sabrina explained again, "The third hotel is run down, it has running water some of the time, but it does not have electricity all the time, and it has a smell to greet you." The two argued, "We can do better without electricity than we can without running water." "That is right! At least we will be able to take a shower and flush the toilets." Sabrina reminded them, "If you have not forgotten, this is the tropics. No electricity. No air conditioner. No fan. No lights. Sure, let's go!" The two ladies hung their heads down low. "This is going to be the most miserable time of our lives." "It sure is!"

As Amy finished cutting the grass, she was smiling with glee. "He is so cute! Could he really like me? I know why Pa thinks I would want a guy like that."

As dawn broke, the clouds were heavy in the sky. It really did not look like rain just yet. The day was already warm for it never cooled off – it just became a little less hot. The five tourists with their guide were walking together.

They came upon the busiest intersection in town. On one of the corners was a large tin of fruit with a cloth. Protruding were pineapples, bananas, cucumbers, and tomatoes. Everyone ignored it just like it did not exist. Sabrina asked their guide, "Why is that bucket of fruit there?" "Someone is trying to appease the spirits. Bad things have happened. The fruit is an offering to the spirits so that they will remove the curse." Sabrina posed another question, "Why don't people just take the fruit?" "Who wants to steal from the spirits? No one wants to be cursed."

Mickey asked Red, "Tell me why we go all the way to Africa to go to church?" Red answered, "This is one of the many grandchildren churches started by the missionaries. Mickey said, "Tell me about them. What made them so special!" Red responded, "That is not a question that can be responded to directly." Mickey answered, "What kind of answer is that except an adult answer where they don't think kids will understand." Red laughed, "We do that enough, but not in this case! How do you look inside of someone who has been long since dead?" Red looked up and saw everyone entering this very bland-looking hut. "We ran out of time. Maybe next time I will tell you more about the missionaries!" "So, you won!" "What do you mean?" "You wanted to end at a good spot in the story to drive me crazy, and you did!"

The building was not a church building at all. The reunion place was an average size hut. The walls were coated in clay. The interior was very dark for the walls were sealed without windows and one small light hung near the stage. The stage was not a stage at all, but there was a pulpit. Whoever lived there had emptied their house of all they owned. There were a few benches. Most people who came in were carrying their own plastic chairs. The kids came in and sat on four benches. The benches were about ten feet long. No toddlers were whining or playing in the dirt. Even the little ones did not have the terrible attitudes found in children aged two or three. The bigger kids kept pulling more and more smaller ones on their laps. The heat was increasing rapidly as the bodies entered the building. The kids did not gripe about the heat. Body against body they crammed in. On three sides, the young'uns have full body contact, yet none of these kids pushed or hit one another. Many kids just stood one by the other. By the time the service had started, those four benches contained sixty kids.

In contrast, the space between the stage and the pulpit was large. Red was wondering, why make all the kids sit and stand so close together and waste a third of the building up front? The adults squeezed their chairs just as closely together as they could. Even the handles of the chairs overlapped so as to not waste space. By the time the service started, there were forty-five adults. The building was more the size of a large bedroom about ten yards by six yards. Yet all the people were squeezed into two-thirds of the space. The heat from the torsos was so overpowering that Red began to sway. Not one person grumbled about the heat. It was hot, but complaining had been forsaken.

Two benches faced the center aisle – there mostly sat women. Red gathered correctly that it was the choir. What he was about to see next was a little shocking. The choir not only sang loudly, but they were … as the thought popped into his mind that they were dancing. He quickly corrected himself. This is a choir, they are doing it together, choreography! was the new term. That's right, this is not dancing, this is choreography! After a little bit, the whole church was singing. All the women were in choreography. They were all dancing. Red looked some more. All the kids were in rhythm as well. Only half the men were stomping and shaking to the music. Red did not know what to think. Red was definitely uncomfortable with the synchronized rhythm of the church. The people were singing loudly with all their hearts.

All of a sudden, a lady left her seat dancing as she went. Another lady followed in full rhythm. Soon, there was a circle of ladies dancing up front together in rhythm. Red was really uncomfortable with all the dancing in the church. Red was convinced that they were trying to draw attention to themselves. Red kept staring. What else was he to do? He did not understand the language. He noticed that they all had the same basic footwork. They all did the same. No one was trying to out-fancy the others. He began to feel ashamed. They were not trying to draw attention to themselves for the dancing was a corporate thing. Red realized he had misjudged them.

Red looked around the room. He heard the sound of drums. Someone was beating an African drum. He looked some more, but there was not a guitar. Surely, there was a keyboard. Red could not find one. Red continued to think, that maybe it was because this building did not have electricity. He looked up, and there was a weakly glowing lightbulb. No instruments were there except for the one drum. Maybe, he thought to himself, maybe there was no one to teach them how to play. Then the thought dawned on him. If no one can teach drums, keyboarding, or guitar, then no one has one. The understanding of poverty set in. The lack of basic goods jolted him. They did not have much. They borrowed a house for a building – a house that was too small. They didn't have instruments except for a handmade drum. After seeing the extreme poverty, Red understood the need for dancing. The tiny room was dark, and scorching, with no musical instruments except for a drum. They had so little going for them, but the room was full of life. The ladies dancing combined with the great vigor of people singing brought so much life to the service.

Right before the preaching, a man called Red forward. Red was not expecting this. The man asked Red in English, "Why did you come?" "I came because I wanted to know God more." All responded with a loud, "Amen!" "I had heard that God was moving with great power here. I long to see God in others, so I came. I did not understand what was said, but I saw extreme boldness as you sang and danced. The first Christians among you have the reputation of risking their lives for the Gospel. Can I see with my own eyes how many of you risked everything for the Gospel?" Some stood immediately. Others were called out to stand. "Thank you for your testimony! I needed to see it. The reason you were and are still so bold is that your hearts burn for God and for those around you. You risked it all; and as a result, many more are here. That is why we came. We are here to testify of the ones God loves." The people gave a hearty, "Amen!" Red pointed to Sabrina, "Sabrina organized the trip. She is writing an article about you and your founders." Red motioned for Sabrina to come and he slowly made his way back to his seat. Somehow as he spoke his feet had gone numb and were tingling. He thought to himself, "You would not think that speaking to a bunch of strangers would be so intense that the body would shut off most of the blood to the extremities, but it does."

Quickly, Sabrina found the front. "I am writing an article on your founding fathers, and the churches that have sprung from it. I am wanting to know why you are different, and how you are different. The first believers immediately risked their lives after hearing about Jesus. Why did they do it? How hard is that flame burning now?" The pastor walked up beside her and spoke, "We don't know much about the missionaries or even the first Christians. We are a fourth-generation church. Our missionaries started a church, which then started a church. Out of the second church came another church. The third-generation church then started us. We have never met anyone who knew them. We never even have had missionaries here." Sabrina simply responded, "Oh!" The pastor continued, "We did not know why we are different from a lot of the churches around. It is common for churches to not even try hard to reach people for Jesus, but our hearts pound for those around us! God's love won't let us ignore them. Our hearts break for them. We did not know that the founders' hearts burned for the lost and that the first Christians also paid such a big price. Maybe you could tell us more!" "I don't know more either. I do know that we came to see those whose hearts burn for God. We see God's passion is alive and well in you."

Outside up against the wall where no one could see them were three figures from the blue car with sinister thoughts. Ma opened her mouth, "I don't believe this! We have come halfway around the world to hear people talk about Jesus." Gene continued the thought, "We have come even to kill to gain the true power of this land. Nothing is going to stop us from gaining the magical ripple here." Gus adds, "We have terrified and hurt many people. These people are willing to lose their lives without fear to care about strangers. Imagine that! Have you ever seen anyone willing to die for us?" Ma responded, "Naw! People have always been terrified of us!" Gene jumped in, "That is right, we are people's worst nightmares! They fear us!" All of a sudden, Ma and Gene started talking much louder to each other. Gus exhorted, "Shh! I can't hear!" Ma and Gene responded together, "We don't want to listen that is why we are talking louder!" Gus countered, "But maybe I do!" Ma attacked, "You have always been much too mushy!"

Amy was pouring milk into her cereal and spoke out loud, "Never in my life has any guy been so bold and so cunning all at the same time. Zach kept telling me how pretty I was, and how pleasing I would be. I did not realize how many compliments he gave."

She paused for a moment. "He pretended not to be interested in me but kept telling me how amazing I am. Never has anyone ever been … been … so … fanatic about me. And I was not even aware of what he was doing. I'm so clueless."

Amy took a bite and chewed. She took another bite and ground the next mouthful to nothing. "I still can't call him."

The church members eagerly walked the five a little way down the road, only to later follow a trail. There was a clearing. The translator spoke, "We have cleared off the land. We have laid the foundation." The walls were made of brick and about waist high. The building was not really much bigger than where they were meeting. In fact, by the time they complete it, all may not fit inside. Rather than being frustrated that the building was too small, they were very excited about their land and budding building for they finally would have a place of their own.

Once they arrived at the church construction site, the men were seen stirring a large amount of cement with shovels for they did not have electric cement mixers. They were mixing the heavy powder with sand. The women arrived with buckets of water on their heads to mix the water with the cement the men were mixing. They dumped the water only to make another trip. They carried the water for lack of water hoses. Within the church building, the ground was not level. To level the land, the women were carrying dirt on their heads because they did not have a tractor to haul and level the ground. Still, in another area, the men were packing the cement in brick molds. After the molds were stuffed, the men lifted the heavy molds and dropped them many times to settle the cement, then they would turn the molds upside down. Gingerly, the men lifted the mold off the brick.

Zach was sitting in a chair by himself. He arose and headed toward the door, "Amy did not call! If she does not call after church, she will not call!" He looked at his phone, "C'mon call!"

Amy was wearing an elegant dress. One that seemed to have been made just for her. She arose and headed toward the door. She stared at her phone as she strolled! "No, I will not call him." She slid the phone back into her purse.

Mickey and Red were leaving the hotel with the nets and butterfly cages. Mickey asks, "Do you think we will be able to return the butterfly nets?" "Sure, he must be eager to get his nets back." They tried to find a translator. They asked, "Do you speak English?" In the African extreme courtesy, the first person responded, "Anglais? Non! Viens!" The young man guided them to a house. The locals rattled off in an African dialect. The conversation seemed to expand and many others join in. A loud, "Hein!" echoed from someone about 15 yards away, then the previous conversations continued. The guy who led them just waited.

Red was thinking that this was just a lost cause and started to move away. Their leader spoke out, "Attend!" while he was raising the hand with the palm out, fingers were spread to signal stop. Mickey asked Red, "Do you know what is going on!?" Red responded gruffly, "You can't ask that question!" Mickey was confused about why Red sounded mad, for Red was always mellow. Red spoke out, "You can't ask that question! That is my question to ask you. Do you know what is going on?" "For a moment, I thought you were mad at me!" "Wonderful!" "Wonderful? Wonderful that I thought you were mad at me?" "Precisely!" Mickey punched Red in the stomach. Red dropped to one knee. He curled his arms around his abdomen and grunted, with shortness of breath, "Ah, ah, ah, ah, ah, ah, ah!" Mickey just stood there not knowing what to do. All of a sudden, Red stood up straight and smiled. Mickey just belted Red harder in the same spot. Without realizing it, everyone gathered around and saw the episode. The whole crowd erupted in laughter. Red was not done acting, this time he backed up as fast as he could like the punch had hurled him.

A man walked up, and their young guide pointed at him. This newcomer expressed, "How can I help you?" Red responded, "We are trying to find the hotdog salesman!" The man was greatly puzzled, "You are wanting to me to show you someone who sells dogs that are hot?" Mickey responded, "Hotdogs to eat?" "The man responds, "You're hungry! I know just the place where the food is perfect for you." "No, we want the man who sells hotdogs." "What is a hotdog?" "It is a piece of meat kind of like this." Mickey pressed the fingertips of both hands together in a circle the size of the roundness of a hotdog, then he pulled his hands apart to show the length while he was still keeping the circular shape. "It is a piece of meat." "What kind of meat?" "You can't tell by looking at it, but usually it is either beef or pork!" "Are you trying to say that a hotdog is either cow or pig, but not dog?" "That is correct!" "Can you explain it a little more?" "It comes on a bun." "A bun?"

At that time, another man strolled up, and spoke, "I ate with an American once! I know what a hotdog is, but we do not have hotdogs around here." Red protested, "But, I saw him right over there!" He pointed adamantly at a spot not too far away. He had a hotdog cart. The newcomer states, "A cart – a fancy American food vending stand on wheels." Red and Mickey both got really excited, "Yes, yes, yes, yes!" The deflating response came, "No one here sells food from a cart!" The first translator spoke as an expert, "No, we do not have rolling food carts here. No one has ever seen one in this village." "Are you hungry?" Mickey answers in a discouraged voice, "No!" Red responded, "You are so kind. Thank you for your help!" They both nodded with a slight bow. In unison, the two translators responded, "Of course!" Red turned to Mickey, "Do you want to hunt more butterflies?" "Yeah!"

In the background was a church. Zach looked at his phone and said as he unlocked his car, "If she has not called by now, she won't call! I could call her, but I can't. I had told her like four times, how pretty she was, and said how fabulously incredible she is. All she said was I didn't want to call you and don't get any ideas. I can't call her!" Slowly he slid the phone back into his pocket. He opened the door in silence. He sat down, cranked the car, and closed the door without saying another word.

Amy was home and opened the refrigerator door as she was looking for something to eat. She announced, "I was tricked yesterday, He kept saying how pretty I was, and even talked like I was the best person ever, and I didn't even realize all the wonderful things he was saying. That kind of guy is a keeper."

Mickey's aunt and Grandmother were both wondering, "How are we going to flush the toilet?" To the side was a huge bucket that looked more like the bottom half of a barrel than it did a bucket. The aunt tried to lift it up and with her arm locked was able to pick the bucket up off the floor. "This bucket is heavy!" "It sure is!" I don't know how we are going to flush." "I don't either." "If we dump the water in the toilet, how do we know when enough is enough?" "We don't want to waste the water either." "Oh, no, no, no, no!" By now both women have gripped the bucket. "Are you ready?" "I am ready! Are you ready?" "Ready!" "Do you want to just lift it up or do you want to go on the count of three?" "Oh, that is a good question. We could on the count of three or we could just lift it up." "Let's count …" "Before she had the opportunity to finish the sentence, the other joined in." "Together!" "One, two, three!" They lifted up the bucket and tilt it until the water was at the brim and they stopped. "Do you know how much we need to turn this contraption?" "It does not come with instructions!" "That it does not!" "Not those instructions would be of much use to us!" "They would be in another language anyway!" "The man should have shown us how to flush the toilet." "He should have, but do you think …" "Yeah, it is pretty silly of a man to show us how to flush the toilet." "It is getting heavy!" "I was thinking the same thing." Are you ready?" "Ready!" They started pouring water into the toilet. To avoid wasting water, they barely tilted the bucket, and a very small stream of water flowed over the edge. "That looks more like a pee stream than a flush." "Pssssst!" They both bust out laughing, and set the bucket down.

Red and Mickey headed toward the exit. They were passing the woman's door and heard the laughter. Mickey confessed, "I have never heard my aunt and grandmother laugh like that!" "Do you want to ask them what is so funny?" "No, we will hear that story many times – many, many times." They continued out the hallway that was too narrow for them to walk side by side.

Zach was sitting on the edge of his bed just sad. He muttered to himself in a beat voice, "She drives me crazy! Why am I even interested in a gal who made it very clear she will have nothing to do with me? I don't know what to do. I guess I will just sit here and be miserable." He giggled softly at himself.

Amy was pacing from one end of her bedroom to another. "This is exactly why I desired for nothing to do with Pa's boy. He would be charming … cute … and maddening. I knew I should never have called him."

CHAPTER 5
THE ADVENTURE BEGINS

As Red and Mickey approached the edge of the field, they noticed the same three from yesterday standing in the middle of the field. Both Red and Mickey stopped. Mickey spoke, "They make me feel uncomfortable!" "Let's just stay away from them and catch our butterflies." Mickey declared, "I know what we will call these butterflies, 'Lightning Strikes!' They are totally black and they look like lightning all over their wings." "Good name! From the guy who gave us the nets, his cart had paintings of these butterflies and lightning bolts all over."

Gene declared, "That old man knows something! Why else do you go halfway around the world and hang out in this field twice?" Ma agreed, "I am sure of it. He brought butterfly nets just to give him an excuse to hang out in this field. It just makes no other sense." By now, Gus was just ready for something else to happen, "So what are you going to do about it?"

By then, the butterfly catchers were really good at catching the butterflies. Mickey spotted a fluttering black and yellow. He gently moved the net under the butterfly with the mouth opened upwards. He raised the net until the weightless creature continued its dance within the confines of the belly of the net. Quickly, he spun the handle. The butterfly was trapped in the bottommost part of the net that was hanging over the side of the brim. The expert pulled in the handle until he had secured the ring in one hand. With the other, he slowly slid his hand into the net. With much care, he wrapped his fingers around the butterfly. He left a cupped hollow as large as he could without leaving a hole big enough for the creature to escape. He felt the wings tickling his palm. He removed the net from his hand and slid the pole between his thighs. Red held the butterfly cage directly in front of the lad. Mickey placed his fist on the entrance of the cage. He opened his fingers until the butterfly was wedged between a cupped palm and the door of the box. The door to the cage was nothing more than a circular piece of wood held in place by one nail at the top. With the index finger, on the other hand, he spun the flap 180 degrees so that the butterfly could float into the opening. Red declared, "Look at you! You make it look so easy."

Red revealed the start of butterfly hunting, "Monkabe told me that catching the butterflies would be the beginning of an adventure." "An adventure! Just the beginning of an adventure? Awesome!" "Yes, this has made great entertainment, but a poor adventure!"

What was not seen during this time was the approaching of the three devious ones. Gene declared, "I told you that he knew something about this place!" Ma in triumph, "You sure did! They have a lot of explaining to do!" Red questioned, "Explaining about what?" "Ma dug, "About this adventure of yours!" Red corrected, "There is no adventure!" Ma pushed harder, "No adventure, plah, you're lying! You just said the word adventure. Red retorted, "I stand corrected. Now the adventure begins, I am being accused of lying!" Gene started over, "Why are you out here in this field?" Red responded simply, "I am out here in this field to catch butterflies. Can you think of a better way to spend an afternoon here in Africa when there is nothing to do, and I can't talk the language?" Gene questioned, "Why did you choose this field?" Red gave an obvious answer, "Look around, everywhere else there are trees!" Red looked in all directions, but no one else looked around. Gene gave an ultimatum, "You are going to tell us what you know?" Red responded, "I am happy to tell you what I know. This is a great field to catch butterflies. I wish I could tell you more, but I can't."

Ma upped the stakes, "I like your boy! He must be very precious to you!" Mickey did not like innuendos that he might get hurt, "His boy? I am not his boy! I never did anything with him till yesterday." "The whole market was laughing at me because my mom tried to buy me a fertility doll. Like I am going to get pregnant." Gene interrupted, "Whoa, whoa, whoa, whoa, enough about that doll. What do you know about lightning and teleportation?" Red asked, "Teleportation – like being beamed from one place to another?" Gene affirmed, "Yeah, that kind of teleportation where in an instant, you are zapped from one place to another. What do you know?" Red gave an unsatisfactory answer, "All I know is the comic book stuff. The kind of thing superheroes is made of." Gene informed, "We are not talking about comic book heroes. We are talking about what happens in this field during lightning storms." Mickey jumped in, "Cool, so you are trying to tell me that teleportation really exists? In this very field?"

Ma gentled and squatted so that she was Mickey's height, "Yes, teleportation happens in this very field during lightning storms. You can be looking across this field and see no one, and the next moment, someone is close enough to lick your nose. Then just like that. (She snaps her fingers.) Just like that, a stranger is in your face, the next moment gone again." Red protests, "That kind of power does not exist!" Gene sets things in order, "Don't kid yourself, too many people like yourselves have seen it throughout the centuries. This phenomenon is for real."

All this time, Gus had remained silent, "You are free to leave." Anger flared in Gene's voice, "He is going to tell us." Gus confirmed, "Of course, he is going to tell us! Maybe he knows, maybe he doesn't! But whoever sent him out in this plot to catch butterflies wants him to figure it out. He will know before he leaves." Ma lights up, "Good thinking! Don't say, I never said anything nice about you!" Gene made it final, "You can leave, but don't think you can leave this village without telling us."

In front of the toilet stood two ladies. "Are you ready to try flushing this toilet again?" "Oh, absolutely! We need to figure this thing out." "That is right, we will not ask that man to show us how to flush the toilet." "We are capable!" "At our speed, we will need to flush it again …" The two finish the sentence together, "before we flush it the first time!" They both laughed. "One!" "Two!" Then together, "Three!" They lifted up the bucket and poured plenty of water down the toilet. "We did it!" "We flushed the toilet!" "Do you see anything down there?" "Oh, I don't! Do you?" "Neither do I!" Together, "We flushed the toilet!"

An African couple entered the gate of the hotel. There in the shade of a tree outside sat Sabrina. There was a mango tree out of season. All along the wall was a row of papaya trees loaded down with yellow to green papayas. The shade tree was a big leafed sturdy tree that she had been told was an avocado tree. The African couple greeted Sabrina with incredible kindness. "We are so thankful that you have come! You being here means a whole lot to our church! Knowing that somebody was willing to leave a nice life to go halfway around the world to see God here touches us deeply." "Thank you."

Sabrina expressed, "We saw you sing and dance with all your hearts. Knowing the price of Christianity here, you have touched us deeply." "God is good! Others all over the area have heard about your coming. A chief in another village has invited many Christians from all around the region for you to pray for them. They want you to come now and talk to them before they all leave. Many more from other churches are gathering so that they will meet you." "Right now?" "Yes, right now! They want to see you before they have to leave. God has never sent missionaries to them before." "But we are not ready to leave." "They have a place for you to stay! Go! Go now!"

Mickey and Red were walking back into the village. Mickey asked, "Why did you not tell me about all this teleportation?" "I did not know, but the man who gave me these butterfly nets knows the legends!" "How do you know?" "He had lightning and faces drawn all over his cart." Mickey was astonished, "You mean the one who sent you out told you that your adventure is beginning is an expert on the mystery!" "That's right!" Mickey declared in astonishment, "Your adventure is teleportation! You are going to have great power to jump from one place to another in a snap."

Zach was just staring at the clock. "I thought I had caught her. Instead, she caught me and doesn't even want me! It is like when you go fishing and catch a snake. You can't unhook the poisonous tube, but you don't want it either. It's hopeless!"

Amy was making a list of what she needed to buy from the store. "Pa will be here, and I need to figure out what food to buy. Of course, corn on the cob, chicken with … I will be glad when Pa gets back. When Pa gets here, things will go back to normal. We will do stuff, cook together, go for walks, talk, and I won't have the time to think about that nuisance boy of his."

Sabrina opened the door slightly to her mother's and sister's room. "Can I come in?" "Sure!" "Sure!" "C'mon in!" The two were walking around the tiny room looking for something. They picked things up and shuffled things around. Sabrina asked, "What are you looking for?" "We flushed the toilet!" "We sure did!" "It was quite an adventure!" "We spilt a lot of water on the floor and we are trying to find a way to clean it up." "That is right, a lot of water!" "There is nothing to dry the floor with except our own towels. If we dry the floor with our towels, then what will we dry ourselves with when we take a shower?" "Let me solve that problem for you, you are not taking a shower because we are leaving right now. Pack your stuff, we are leaving." "Leaving?" "Leaving right now?" "We can't leave! We have to clean the floor!"

Sabrina interrupted their saga, "The whole bathroom is made of tile! It was made to be hosed down and wet!" "Oh!"

Red invited Mickey, "Come over here! This is where I met the man who started all this." Red kept approaching, but for no reason for nothing was there! There was not even a hotdog stand. The market was empty. Mickey, "I don't see anyone!" "He is not here!" "So, what do we do?" "I don't know!" "You don't have any idea?" "No, but this is exactly what an adventure is! You have no clue what you are doing, but you are certain it is something big!"

At a distance behind, the three were following. Gus boasted, "See, I told you we should let them go! They are searching for someone. They will know who to contact. It is only a matter of time now, and we will know!"

Mickey and Red resumed their walk back to the hotel! Red pondered out loud, "The third guy who did not say much till the end – I am not sure I have him figured out. He did not attack us like the other two." "I noticed that as well. It was almost like he was trying to protect us, but he had such a devilish plan." "I could not figure out if he was trying to protect us or tightening the noose around our necks."

Gene declared, "They are in a rush to figure this out for us!" Ma relished, "This plan is coming together!"

CHAPTER 6
TELEPORTATION

The sun had then set, and a vehicle was driving up toward them. With the village being so very dark, the headlights seemed to be blinding. The car was moving slowly. Mickey asked, "Can you tell who it is?" "No!" "I just hope it is not more crazy Americans who are eager to hurt us." The van continued to pull past them. All of a sudden, the window slid down, and the van came to a complete stop. A female voice yelled, "Hop in!" Both guys moved toward the sliding door. Red lifted up the cage and noticed that a butterfly was dead. He called out, "Just a moment, let me throw this dead butterfly out!"

Red walked to the ditch to cast out the dead critter. Once he arrived, he carefully opened the cage so as not to let the butterflies escape. He carefully inserted two fingers into the cage. Many butterflies gracefully flapped into his hand. He tilted the cage so that the dead butterfly would have been easily accessible to the wandering fingers. He did not feel the butterfly so he tilted the cage some more. So many butterflies were in this cage that he continually felt the flapping of the wings. Finally, the butterfly laying on the bottom was close enough to pick up using the two fingers within the cage. Red squeezed the butterfly between his inserted fingers, and all of a sudden Red realized he lost it.

The light was poor, but a new light was coming as well – a motorcycle was rattling his way. Red moved directly into the beam of the motorcycle so that he could see. Once in the light, he had a clear look inside the cage. He looked and the dead butterfly had vanished from the bottom. He shook the cage a little. He still could not find the dead butterfly. He muttered to himself, "I know the butterfly was dead. Surely, it did not wake up and start flying all over again."

Ten seconds later, he realized the light of the motorcycle was still shining directly on him. He looked up. The motorcycle was perfectly still. He peered at the legs of the driver. Although hard to distinguish, the legs were firmly resting on the footrests. "How can this motorcycle be completely still without moving forward and the feet on the pedals? How long can he hold it? One, two, three, four, five, six, seven!" He realized that counting was pointless for the motorcycle was frozen.

In a surprise, Red hopped back and the motorcycle immediately resumed humming down the road at the same cozy speed as before. As the driver approached, Red waved to the driver. In return, the conductor smiled and lifted his hand off the handlebars and waved. With the raising of the arm to wave, the man on the machine ever so slightly wobbled the handlebars. The moving light beamed upon Red and chased away the shadows. Just like before the motorcycle stopped as if frozen.

Red laughed to himself, "This must be the secret of teleportation. Except, I am not being teleported very fast for I am going nowhere." He looked down at the driver's feet once again. His legs were propped up on the footrests and as before he was absolutely still. That motorcycle looked more like a photograph, not a moving vehicle. Red stepped back into the shadows, and the motorcycle resumed humming again. Immediately, Red leaned forward, and the motorcycle stopped.

Red slowly dropped his hands holding the cage into a relaxed position. Red was not even aware of what he was doing for his mind was racing so fast trying to figure out the secret of teleportation. The cage rotated and the butterflies were soon engulfed in the shadows. Immediately, the motorcycle began moving again. Red instantly raised the cage to its previous position. The motorcycle halted once again.

Red snapped his head back and smiled, "I get it! The butterflies need to be in the light to freeze everything." His fingers were still in the cage from trying to remove the vanished butterfly. While keeping the cage in the light carefully he removed his fingers to keep the butterflies from escaping. Immediately, the motorcycle birthed moving again. He yanked his fingers back in. By now, the cyclists had corrected the wobble in his path; and as a result, the light was further away from Red. Red expected the motorcycle to stop, but it did not. He looked down and realized that his hand was no longer illuminated. He lurched forward and encountered the light once again. Just like before everything stopped.

Red looked at his fingers and saw a soft yellow glow where he had touched the dead butterfly. "My fingers are glowing." He pulled his fingers out of the cage, well almost, but ceased because he did not wish to let his fingers even briefly be in the dark. He attempted removing just his middle finger, but the opening was just too small. He gave up on that finger and focused on the index finger. He endeavored to free the index finger. He almost had it, but it too could not escape the cage and stay in the light. With all the speed he could muster, he jerked his fingers out. The motorcycle moved two inches and halted again.

Red shut his hand; the motorcycle resumed speed. He opened his hand and the cycle stopped once more. Three times, Red closed his hand and unfolded it. When the fingertips were out of the light, the motorcycle regained normal speed. Each time the light caught his fingers as he opened his hand, the two-wheeler froze.

Slowly, he pulled the cage backward drawing it out of the light while keeping his fingers in the head beam. Nothing happened. The caged butterflies seemed to have no power at all. Several times, he swung them like a pendulum in and out of the light, but the living butterflies had no effect on the motorcycle.

Red continued his experiment. He placed the cage back in the light and closed his fingers. Immediately, the cycle lurched forward. Red sprung his fingers open again, and the motorcycle ceased to move. Red declared, "Teleportation, my foot! I still have to walk while everything else halts. Just like the three told me, 'In a flash, someone can appear out of nowhere and be close enough to lick and then disappear.'" Red maintained his fingers clearly in the beam while he was walking ever so closely to the motorcyclist. The noses drew closer together. Finally, when all but the minimal possible space existed before touching happened. Red stopped. In triumph, "I am close enough to lick him. I could slap a wet tongue on his face. Nahn!"

Red slid one step backward. Ever so slowly, Red repositioned his fingers to the edge of the light, then he halted as if to make up his mind. In the reverse direction, the fingers crept back to the center of the light. Without notice, Red yanked his hand back. The driver awoke and saw Red's face ever so close to his. The pilot zoomed by while he was screaming in terror, "Rahh!" It only took a little fear to convert an expert motorcyclist into a novice. The driver jerked his bike, and it wobbled back and forth. The driver doubled his terror for he had lost control of his vehicle. As the pattern of rocking back in forth increased, the motorcyclist demonstrated skill by tapping the ground with his foot just enough to steal some loss of control. The waving motion of the cycle ended and the cyclist gunned the engine to race away. Red declared, "The legend is to appear out of nowhere and get in licking distance to surprise people. I did just like those of old, I teleported out of nowhere – sorta. Glad you did not get hurt, my friend – the motor man."

Off in the shadows were three observers positioned where they couldn't be seen. They began to chatter, "What was that?" "I don't know! Do you?" "I don't either." "What happened, it was like the old-timey films where a few pictures had been damaged and removed creating a glitch." "Did we see something or was the light too bad?" "I don't know!" "But since we all saw it; something must have happened."

Red looked back at the car. Sabrina had turned around backward and was talking to her sister and mother. "Good!" he muttered, "They did not see a thing." He walked back toward the other side of the car to get in. As he passed the first headlight, Red held out his fingers. He watched Sabrina talk with her hands wildly jumping all over the place. As soon as his fingers crossed the light, the motion ended, and she was suspended. Red paused one moment directly against the front bumper between the headlights.

Back in the shadows, the rambling continued, "He did it again!" "I saw it clearly this time!" "He teleported!" "He did not go very far!" "Two feet!" "Two feet is two feet." "Not very impressive distance-wise, but he figured it out." Ma declares, "We're in bu..."

Once again, she became a statuette as Red crossed the second beam. He was totally unaware of the dark places. Red stared again at a motionless Sabrina with her hair floating and her hands in crazy positions. Red was surprised to hear a familiar voice. "You have come here to Africa to feel alive." Red knew who it was without even looking.

Red placed his fingers directly on the car over the light to keep them from slipping into darkness. He turned around. In front of him was Monkabe. "Your journey has begun. You came to find life again, but the hunt will cost you everything. Learn from butterflies, and you will live." "What do you mean, 'Learn from the butterflies and you will live?' The butterflies are not exactly talking." "You can only learn to hear through the journey!" "I need more help than that. Some very dangerous people are hunting me down!" "Turn around and go!" Red just stood there. "Turn around and go!" Red rotated and walked away from the light. Predictably, Sabrina animated again. Red turned back around, and Monkabe had vanished. "He came and went like nothing happened." A mixed wonder settled over Red. A heaviness because he knew the journey would cost everything and a thrill because the journey had begun.

"...'siness!" Ma blurted out as she became unfrozen. "We are definitely in business!" "Teleportation will soon be ours and we can rob anyone!" "Anywhere!" "At any time, as we please!" "We will become the greatest bandits of all times!" In their gloating, they forgot to notice that Red was entering a vehicle. "Hey, he is getting away!" They rushed forward, but the door closed and the vehicle strolled away!

Ma screamed, "You let our teleporter get away! You two are so incompetent! I can't believe I have to live with you! You are absolutely terrible!" Gene regained his senses, "Relax, we will find him again. At one point, only two roads lead back to the capital city. We will be there waiting." "Yeah, but which one?" "The other one that is out of the way!"

Sabrina's sister crawled all the way back to the dreaded seat. "I will ride back here all the way so Mickey does not!" Red slid in beside Mickey. The lad spoke softly so as not to be heard by the others, "You figured it out. You teleported in that motorcyclist's face. That was so incredibly awesome! He nearly peed in his pants!" "It felt weird to appear in his face out of nowhere." You did mini jumps in front of the car. Those were ... well ... were rather weak." "Trying to figure things out." "Tell me! How did you do it?" Red thought about Monkabe's words that it will cost you everything! Red responded indirectly, "The bandits out there – they will catch up to us again." "So that is a no or are you just trying to change the subject?" "That is most definitely a no." "When the bandits catch up to us again, you could just teleport us away!" "You can't teleport away forever!" "Then they will hunt you down till they kill you!" Red sarcastically teased, "What a great adventure – to be hunted down and killed!"

Zach was pacing faster than before, "I can't wait till Red returns so that he can have me over to the house as he promised. What do I tell him? "Red, you are so right! Your daughter is incredibly beautiful and … and. Yeah right! That is not going to work!"

Amy tried to reason with herself,

> "Dad can't come home soon enough! Oh wait, he will ask about Zach, 'Did you call Zach? He is a great young man, isn't he?' How do I answer that – he is the perfect man for when I am ready for one. He would just smile and say, 'See, I told you that you would like him.' Now, I am not wanting dad to return for he is going to bring up Zach. I know he is just not going to bring him up, but he is going to bring him here. I just know it!"

Zach, "Red hurry up and get here!"

Amy, "Dad, please take your time, pleeease!"

CHAPTER 7
THE MASK

The blue car was inching to a stop. "Which way do you think we ought to go now to find them?" asked Gene. Gus questioned, "Do you hear that?" "Hear what?" "The big ruckus." "The only big ruckus I hear is your belly." "You are so right that you can hear my belly, it does not have a massive layer of soundproofing insulation." Ma, "Gene, what happened to you? With all your soundproofing, it would seem like whatever happens in your belly would be the world's best-kept secret."

Gene sought to change the subject and said, "I hear it now, it is coming from that way!" They rolled down the windows to listen. "Maybe someone else is putting on a show for runaway teleporters. They followed the music just like a pied piper was calling them.

A man ran up to the driver's side window shaking baby dolls. Ma, "Oh, how sweet. They are selling baby dolls. Gene, you need to buy one." "What for?" comes the puzzling request. "Buy one for Gus!" Gene adds, "You are so right, Ma. Gus needs his first-ever girlfriend." Ma continued, "A baby doll is not much, but it is much more than he ever had." Gus retorted, "How can I ever have a girlfriend for you two are scarier than a double barrel shotgun."

They drove on a few yards, and another man sprinted up with a baguette in his hand. Gene yelled, "Oh goody, I'm hungry." Gus contradicted, "We do not need a baguette!" Ma yelled, "You are just sore about that baby doll." Gene gloated, "Poor little boy needs his baby doll!" Gus snapped back, "Oh, I had already forgotten about the baby doll stuff. A baguette is super hard on the outside and melts in your mouth on the inside. You, too, are super soft on the outside and flint hard on the inside."

A third salesman dashed to the car. He yelled, « Tu as besoin de ça ! » Gene looked at the electronic gadget and barked, "The last thing we need is an MP3 player singing African chants." The street vendor persisted. He pushed a button, and the gizmo spoke, "You need this!" Gene declared, "A translator!" Ma commanded, "Give me that!" Gene came to a complete stop! All of a sudden, another vendor rushed up to the car; cigarettes! Another, pens! Each yelled to grab their full attention. Within seconds, the car was completely surrounded by salesman two layers thick: toy cars, tomatoes, knives, papayas, t-shirts, cans of sweetened condensed milk, bananas …

The trio arrived at the epicenter of the music. They saw grown men dancing with masks on. The three emerged from the car. Ma led the charge with a gizmo in hand trying to hear and understand. A mother spoke to her child, "Be afraid of them or they will put a terrible curse on you." Another, "They are powerful medicine men!" Ma attempts to be as polite as she can while asking through the translator to a lady with kids around her. "Why are their masks not prettier?" "The masks are ugly! The masks are to strike fear in your hearts." "Fear, why fear?" "You will learn the power of the medicine men!"

Ma pulled up to a very dignified lady, "Are the dancing men bad people?" "Some are! Others are good! The medicine man is our doctor! He knows the secrets to the ancient remedies! He makes medicine for us!" "So why be afraid of the medicine men?" "Some diseases are curses." "Curses?" "Yes, you fall and break an arm. The reason you fell is that someone paid the medicine men to put a curse on you. Bad things will keep happening to you until you pay the medicine man to remove the curse." "That is nonsense! Who would believe that?" "You will! You will believe the power of the medicine men and the spirits."

"Ma, come here! Come, Ma, come!" demands Gene. Ma rushes over. "This weirdo will not let me pass." In front of them was a trail that led into the jungle! Ma rudely asks through the translator, "Why will you not let my son pass?" The masked man replies, "Behind is a sacred forest. If you enter, you will die!" Ma ragged on her son, "Don't you appreciate when a man tries to save your life?" In disgust, Gene pleaded, "C'mon, Ma! Don't be like that!" The man with the overgrown headgear spoke once more, "Only medicine men can enter. All others die!" Gus snickered, "Go ahead Gene, go right in!" Gene spun around and glared. His face burned red from the thought that Gus wished he was dead. Gus continued, "You think that I wish for you to die? Not at all! Go later when it is dark – that is what we do!" Gene calmed down and Gus poked, "I got you, good! Your face was glowing like a super blood moon."

Darkness had settled, and the three emerged in black from head to toe. Even the face was covered with a black ski mask. Ma growled, "We will see how big and tough that man and his curse are now."

The spies reached a bend in the path. Ma was standing behind a tree hiding her body. She leaned her head around just far enough to see what was beyond. Gene and Gus were standing behind her. They both gently backhanded each other's arms to gain one another's attention. They turned and smiled. Gus removed his face mask and knelt directly behind Ma. Gene also crouched and took his position. Gus softly rubbed Ma's ankle with the face mask. In terror, Ma jumped away. Just as Ma started her jump, Gene spread his arms out wide. She landed right in front of Gene where her back was facing him. Gene's hands snapped inwards. They clamped on Ma's leg. His palms slapped her leg hard, and his fingertips dove into the flesh simulating a bite of a big animal. She jumped again. Gus stood up and sucked her in tightly with one arm, and the other covered her mouth to keep her from screaming.

Ma looked around at both boys. They were all contorted with laughter. Ma exclaimed, "How dare you!" Gene triumphantly spoke, "That was the funniest thing ever!" Gus added, "I have never seen you so terrified ever!" Ma defended, "I was not terrified!" Gene continued, "You listened to too many stories of witch doctors and curses." Ma argued, "I was not afraid of the curses! I thought it was a wild animal!" Gene continued what he does best, "Exactly Ma! The wild animal is the curse." "You were sure that one of those men had turned into a beast and was attacking you." Ma opened her mouth to spit out some dignity-saving words. She realized the best solution was to exit the scene so she stormed down the trail. "I would rather be with whatever is down there than be with you!" Gene, "Have you ever heard such thoughtful words from a mother before?" Gus was rubbing imaginary tears out of his eyes, "So touching!"

Ma and the boys soon arrived at a hut. They looked around for signs of life. Gene began, "I don't see anyone!" Gus, "Me neither!" Ma stormed up to the door and opened it. With her flashlight, she peered inside, "C'mon cowards!" The boys hopped up and followed. Ma continued, "Why that is the fastest you, two have ever minded. Maybe there is hope for you after all."

They looked inside the hut. Absent were both bed and cooking materials. Dangling all around the room were the masks the performers wore earlier in the evening. Gene reached above one and found a fishing string. All around the room against the walls were the spears and shields. Gus exclaimed, "This is the dancers' storeroom." Gene declared, "No wonder they did not want us to come."

Gene picked up and unhooked the most hideous mask he could find and put it on his head. Ma finally smiled, "That is the best you have ever looked. You should wear that mask forever." Gus remembered the barbie doll teasing. "If you wear that mask when we return home, you stand a chance of finding a woman." "Women are much more drawn to me than to you!" countered Gene. Ma blurted, "Is that so? I have never seen a hot chick or even a toad pay attention to you!"

CHAPTER 8
THE BABIES AND THE HIPPO

Mickey moaned "When will it stop raining? It has been raining forever." In a much louder tone, Sabrina bellowed, "What? You have to yell to talk over the pounding of the rain on the tin roof." The rain on the roof sounded like ten drum rolls all happening at the same time except each had its own rhythm. Sabrina spoke, "It has been raining for a day and a half." "I'm bored." "Can't you find something to do!" "The butterflies don't fly when it rains." "What else could you do?" "I could go for a walk with Red, but the grass is so wet and itchy." "Anything else, you can think of doing?" "Oh wait! I have a perfect idea; we can go snake hunting!" "Snake hunting? What do you mean, snake hunting? Did I not tell you we are in Africa?"

Two hours later, the rain ceased. Mickey begged, "Mom, can't we go do something?" "Sure!" "There is this place we can go and watch them do chicken sacrifices to the spirits." With eagerness, they all hopped in the van. Ten minutes down the road, they came to a screeching halt. The water was zipping across the road. Before the van could stop, the front wheels entered the water. The water looked like a super thin layer skimming over the road. The flowing appeared innocent enough. Just as soon as the tires entered the flooded area, the front wheels dropped just like they had driven off a curb. The act-a-like mother and daughter, went to squealing, "We are going die!" "We're drowning!" "Someone help us!" "This is the end!" Somehow both ladies were dancing a jig upon their seats.

Sabrina threw the car in reverse, and bolted the car backward! "Oh, that was close!" "We could have died." "You are right about that." "Africa is the scariest place ever!" Continued the women. Red interrupted, "We only dropped five inches." The ladies turned and gave him the death glare. Red wisely continued, "You are right! We do not know how much of the road was washed out. It could have gotten very dangerous quickly!"

Sabrina declared, "The road is blocked, we will need to come up with a different plan." Red suggested, "Why don't we go see the lake? I am sure it will look very different after the rain." Sabrina asked, "Anyone object?"

As they arrived at the water's edge, a large crowd had gathered. They heard screaming, moaning, and harsh commanding. They all hopped out of the car quickly. They recognized a woman who spoke English and raced up to her. "Who drowned?" "Who was it?" "Who's dead?" "Who died?" The African replied, "No one yet!"

They watched a woman softly cradle a baby that was dripping with water. In relief, the just-arrived crew yelled, "The baby is alive!" "The baby made it!" "The child survived!" "Oh, wonderful!" "That was a close call!"

The mother began screaming again in great grief as if the baby had already died. With all her might, she hurled the baby back into the water. Another baby was at the water's edge. Horrified, another mother grabbed her baby and slung the infant back in the water.

On this particular day, a gentle breeze was blowing straight toward the land. The lapping waves gently pushed the baby back toward the shore scooting the little one back to safety.

The whole group of foreigners raced up to the mothers and yelled "Stop!" "Stop!" "Stop!" Pausing long enough to explain things through an interpreter, the mother quickly stated, "One of the babies is an evil spirit!" "We don't know which one is evil!" "We are throwing our babies in so that the spirits will take the evil spirit, then we will know!" Red responded, "You have your answer." Sabrina continued, "Neither baby was taken. Neither is an evil spirit!"

The interpreter explained, "Even if the mothers quit throwing their babies into the water today, they will regret it. The evil spirit will make people get sick and die. Others will pay for keeping the baby alive."

"It is just a little water," claimed Ma. Gene retorted, "Driving through it is crazy." Ma argued, "The water is barely over the road." Gene replies, "I am not concerned how deep the water appears to be, I am concerned how much of the road the flowing water has washed out." Ma snapped, "Prove it! Prove me wrong! Go out in it and prove to me that we cannot drive through that water." Gene retorted, "No, Ma, you go out and see how deep it is!" Ma declared, "How dare you try to send your own Ma into rushing water to be swept away and never to be seen again?" Gene grumbles, "How different is it to send me to never be seen again?"

Gene turns to Gus, "C'mon, let's go check out the water." Gus snapped back, "By us, you really mean me!" Gene "No, I will go in the water with you." Gus, "If you are going in, there is no need for both of us to drown. Go right ahead." Gene informed, "I will hold your hand and if you fall, I will drag you out." Gus declared, "I don't know what is worse: to be dragged along in the current banging against every rock until I drown or to hold your hand!"

All three were standing by the waters. Ma, "Go in Gus!" Gus replied, "Don't you care if I die?" Ma, "Don't be such a baby. Get in!" Gene poked a stick into the water proving the ground had not been washed away. "See, you are all riled up over nothing!" Gus stepped in the water. From the swiftness of the water, the brown gunk splashed up his leg. Ma, "See, it is nothing!" Gus retorted, "If it is nothing, then you step in and test the waters." Gus and Gene made the most terrible faces as they grabbed ahold of each other's hands. Gus kept walking further and further out until their arms were fully stretched. The ground was level and flat. Gus declared, "You are going to have to step in the water for me to go any further."

With his other hand, Gene reached to his midsection and grabbed his belt. He started unhooking his belt to remove it. "What happened to you going into the water with me?" Gene responded, "The footing is better on dry land – better to save your life."

Ma yelled, "Don't take off that belt! If your pants fall, that sight will give me nightmares for as long as I live." With the belt off, Gene began to shake his booty." Ma demanded, "Don't shake your pants off!" Gus declared, "I am better off just drowning now."

While holding on to the belt, Gus kept edging himself out further and further. Ma stated with satisfaction, "See, I told you that the water is harmless!" Gus took another small step, but this time, the ground was not where it should have been. With only one foot planted, the water began pushing the other foot. Unable to keep his balance, Gus toppled over. The water quickly drugs him downstream. The belt snapped tight and neither released their grip. The belt acted like a pendulum and swung Gus close to shore. The flowing water caught Gus' face spraying fiercely upwards. Unable to breathe Gus rolled his way out of the water.

Gus had been attacked by a snorting frenzy. Ma yelled, "You should not have been trying to breathe while underwater!" Gene, "You panicked and breathed! After all these years, you still have not learned the most basic of underwater rules." Gus tried to defend himself before he was ready, and all that was heard was, "Ahrerorui!" Ma yelled, "Speak up, boy!"

After the fit calmed down, Gus declared, "I did everything right! I popped my head up above the water. The rushing water was splashing my face and spraying up my nose. Up my nose, mind you. I would have drowned with my head above water. The only thing that I did wrong, and that was really, really wrong was to listen to you two."

After Gus had regained his composure, he headed back to the car. Ma commanded, "Oh no, you don't!" You are not going to get in the car like that!" Gene declared, "You are covered from head to toe in a brown blackish slime." Gus asked, "Ma, give me something to wipe up with." "I don't have anything!" "Why would you send me in the water if you didn't have anything to wipe me up with?" "You are so wimpy!"

Ma offered a solution, "C'mon, let's go for a walk and you will dry up." After taking only a few steps, they noticed something in the water. Gene announces, "That rushing water uprooted a very large tree." Ma concluded, "To yank such a large tree out of the water, it required serious digging by the water." Gus concluded, "You sent me in water running so fast that it would uproot a large tree and that is somehow, okay?"

All of a sudden, the tree disappeared. Ma exclaimed, "What happened to the tree?" Gene was puzzled as well, "It just sank!" Ma yelled, "Trees don't just sink. How can the rushing water make the tree sink?" Gus declares, "That is not a tree that sank; that is a crocodile!" It was waiting in the rushing water for some poor animal or person to be washed down." Gene announced, "That thing is plenty big to eat you." Gus declared, "The logic of your plans just appears worse and worse. What were you thinking sending me into crocodile-infested waters?"

Since they were still not able to spot the crocodile, Gene advised, "Let's get away from that thing where ever it is." Ma spied a trail by the water flow, "Let's take this trail until you dry up. Eagerly all three ushered down the escape route.

A few minutes later, they heard much screaming and wailing. Their curiosity drove them to the center of the issue. A pirogue was slicing its way to shore. Many were screaming by the shoreside.

Once they saw the three foreigners, many rushed up to speak to them. Ma removed that translator, "A fisherman was out in the rain trying to catch fish. A hippo emerged and flipped the boat. The hippo grabbed the man by the thigh and shook him. Much of his leg is gone. We need your car to take the man to the clinic."

Gene grumped, "We don't have the time for this!" Ma advised, "For a little information on the lost members of our party we do." Gus added in, "They have friends all over. They can tell us where that teleporter is."

Back in the village, the women saw Gus all muddied up. A large group of them grabbed him and drug him away. They took off his shoes, socks, shirt, and pants leaving him with his underwear. Four women were washing him up. Another six washed his clothes. Gene and Ma observed the event. Gus gloated, "Look who has all the women now!"

A man ran up to them, "We have found your friends. They are in a town two hours away." Ma smiled, "See, I told you that we had time to be kind!" Gene commented, "Maybe that road will be passable."

CHAPTER 9
THE ROCK AND THE GREEN MAMBA

The topography was changing. Before, the view was endless tall trees with the underside full of shrubs, ferns, and smaller trees. The grass growth stalled out hip high. The land was absolutely flat – no hill, no mountain, no incline. Without shrubbery and trees to block the view, the flatness of the land was so striking.

Sabrina was driving fairly slowly. She declared, "The location should be about half a mile down the road. Before long, a boulder could be seen on the right side of the road. No other rocks could be seen above the grass line. Out in the middle of seemingly nowhere, a boulder protruded majestically. The round ball of rock seemed so out of place for nothing else was like it.

The day was hot claiming its right as a tropical day; yet at the same time, the day was super cold with the feeling of evil. The place was not any ordinary spot, but one where the evil was just as real as the air itself.

As they approached, they saw three people standing beside the boulder: two men and a woman. One man pulled a chicken out of a cardboard box and handed it to the other man who, in turn, held the chicken down. The woman gave the empty-handed man a machete. With his left hand, he held the chicken's head down to the ground, with the other hand, he cocked back the machete. With one efficient stroke, the machete sliced off the head. The man holding the chicken threw the headless bird high in the air. They counted how many times the headless chicken flapped its wings. One, two, three, four, five, six, seven, and then no more. The chicken lay on the ground lifeless. Even with the chicken immobile, the area was full of energy and everyone screamed in triumph. The couple vigorously shook the hand of the man who threw the chicken up in the air.

The man who brought the chicken walked over to it and scooped it up. He stood in front of the man in charge who reached out and grabbed a few feathers. He yanked to pluck the feathers then he dipped the spines into the accumulated blood at the chopped-off area. The man turned and faced a large square area on the boulder bigger than a square yard. The square was a collection of feathers from previous rituals. To the edge of the square, the feathers were pressed in and held a moment. The blood acting like glue added the feathers to the larger collection. With much eagerness, the man holding the chicken donated it to the witch doctor completing the ceremony. They shook hands one more time, and the couple departed.

Everyone in the car spoke up at once. "What was that?" "What happened?" "Was that some sort of chicken killing ritual?" "That was so gross!" "That is crazy, I did not know that a chicken could keep flopping its wings after losing its head." Sabrina explained, "The couple wanted to know if the spirits would bless their trip with safety. If the chicken flapped the right number of times, then that was the spirits' way of telling the couple that they would have a safe trip."

After departing, no one said anything for ten minutes. Mickey interrupted the silence, "I see a butterfly. Stop!" The whole group welcomed something lighthearted after feeling the power of evil. As soon as they stopped, the young boy jumped out and chased the butterfly. Everyone else oozed out in comparison.

Mickey's aunt and grandmother started a conversation, "Killing a chicken for food is one thing." "But sacrificing a chicken is another." "They are paranoid in fear." "How much more would they have sacrificed if the chicken had not flopped just right?" "Chasing fear is an irrational torture that compounds problems." "We should know." "We are not just cautious with the gloves, masks, and disinfectants." "The worry of catching some disease causes us to" "live in fear" "not enjoy life" and "live in problems" "We are so preoccupied with countless fears that we forget to care about those around us."

Mickey had been listening the whole time, "I am not afraid of anything. I could even catch a poisonous snake." Sabrina corrects, "Rushing into danger in a quest to conquer fear is crazy!" "But Mom, I am not afraid, I can show you have brave I am." "Showing off is not bravery."

Red and Mickey were both standing in an open field looking for more butterflies. The grass reached mid-thigh. Red spoke calmly to Mickey, "Your wish has come true!" Sabrina popped up, "What wish?" Red continued, "Over there, a green snake head is peering over the grass line." Sheer excitement flooded the lad, "Cool!" Sure enough, a green snake head was perched above the grass. With stunning speed, the head popped in each direction surveying the land. Mom declared, "Don't you go after it! You will be grounded! I mean it! Stop don't go! Do you want to be grounded for the rest of your life? I mean it, now!" Even as Sabrina was speaking, the other two women were spewing their opinions as well, "Do you have a death wish!" "Do you want to die today!" "Everyone knows that all snakes in Africa are poisonous." "Don't you dare!"

Ignoring all the threats, Mickey sprinted off toward the snake. At Mickey's first twitch, the snake turned and ran. With the head above the grass line, the snake sped off at a phenomenal speed. Mickey took three steps and stopped for the chase was pointless since the snake ran faster than the lad.

"Stop!" "No!" "What do you think you are doing?" "Get over here right now!" "Mickey Lucas!" yelled the woman. Mickey turned around, "Wasn't that snake so awesome!"

Red prodded, "How were you going to conquer a snake that is 10 times faster than you?" "Just stay away from the snake." "What if it had bitten you?" "You could have died?" "Where is the hospital to take you to?" "We are in Africa!" "You have to think before you act?" "You have to make better choices" bombed the women at Mickey!" Red stated, "That snake could have gone up your shorts and shirt, come out, and bit you on the back side before you reacted. You would have had no chance if that snake chose to bite you."

The women turned their attention to Red. One had the arms crossed; another perched the hands upon hips and the last was shaking a finger at Red. "Don't encourage him to do that!" "It would be all your fault if he got bit!" "I can't believe what you did!"

CHAPTER 10
CHRISTIANITY ORIGEN

Ma rested her hands on her knees while she gasped for air. "I gotta rest for a moment! This running back to the car is … is … just let me catch my breath." Startled Gus asked, "Are you out of breath already?" Ma defended herself, "We ran a long way!" Gene did what Gene did best – he criticized, "We ran only a hundred yards!" Ma raised her voice loudly, "You are overexa … underexag … whatever the right word is, it is a lot farther than one hundred yards." Gus responded, "You see that tree right here! That is the tree we were under!" Ma insisted, "We ran past several trees like that!" Gus corrected, "No, Ma!" Gene declared, "Ma, your memory is worse than your running, and your running is the most pathetic thing I have ever seen! I mean it is stunningly terrible."

Ma handed Gene the keys, "Just go get the car and come get me." Gene took the keys and paused a moment trying to figure things out. He advised Gus, "Why don't you go get the car and come get us? I don't want to leave Ma here by herself." Gus stared at his very large brother, "It looks like you both are exhausted." Gene stuck by his initial reason for staying with his mother, "I wouldn't feel right leaving Ma all by herself here." Gus reminded, "That is not what happened earlier. You thought it was funny to leave Ma at the restaurant shack thing for her to walk back to the hotel."

Thirty minutes down the road, a voice declared, "You have got to stop and let me out of here. I am about to puke. I don't know how Mickey made it thirteen hours back here. Hurry stop!" Mickey and Red stole a look one at another and smiled. Mickey's grandmother called out, "Oh nonsense, riding back there cannot be that bad. I will ride back there and show you." Quickly the vehicle stopped. Long before the vehicle came to a complete stop, "Click!" was heard. Immediately, She bolted up. Her mother, in a very dignified manner with head high and a perfectly straight back, then slid in between the suitcases into the vicious seat.

Zach had been laying on his bed on his back with his hands under his head. Zach grunted, "I got to get busy to get my mind off things!" Zach was unable to move for the invisible prison of love was more powerful than his willpower.

Amy paused a moment to catch her breath. She held a mop in her hands. "I have cleaned all day to get that child out of my mind. I am so tired that I need to rest, but I just can't stop!" Amy would not stop working for the invisible prison of love was forcing much labor.

Another thirty minutes down the road, a voice screamed from the back, "You have got to stop and let me out of here. I am about to puke. I don't know how Mickey made it thirteen hours back here either. It must be because he is young." Red propped his fist out. Very quietly, Mickey gave him knuckles. They both looked at each other and smiled. Sabrina asked, "Can't you make it just a few more minutes, we are almost there?" "No!" came the screech. "Now!" Red extended his fist again and received the same thump as before.

They arrived at the edge of town. Under the first street light, there was a man straddling his motorcycle. The van drew to a stop. The sentry cranked his two-cylinder and weaved around to the driver's side. "Salut!" came the greeting – that ended his attempt to communicate orally. He motioned for them to follow. He twisted his wrist and the bike crunched ahead. The car followed. Very quickly, Sabrina became disoriented for too many turns were made. The trails became thinner. Until there was no trail left suitable for a car. She paused the vehicle and stared. The ruts were driven so deep by the rain that if she attempted, the car would high center. The leader angled sideways and came to a complete stop. He looked back and motioned to the tall grass wall for her to forge through. Sabrina knew that what she had come for is just ahead. She grabbed the stick shift and slid it out of P to D. She forced her transportation into the wall of green. One beam shone brightly; the other was slapped by a continuous carpet of green needles. She had no idea what she was running over. She knew full well that trash was everywhere. The angle of the vehicle was so steep that the passengers started sliding in their seats. To her, it seemed very dangerous, but it was what the locals did; that is if they had a car. Two minutes later, they came upon a building with chairs on the outside because there was not room enough inside.

Enthusiastic chants loudly spilled out of the building. The driver stopped and pulled to the side. Everyone worked their way out of the wheeled cage. Their leader kept motioning, "Come!" They entered the hut. Many were eager to meet them. The visitors took their time and shook everyone's hands. Some of the smallest ones who thought themselves too unimportant to have reached out their hands just stood there staring. The embarrassment of reaching out and being rejected would have felt extreme. The guests took their time and greeted the young ones also. The little faces radiated joy. Their lips split apart into a huge grin revealing white pearls in an otherwise rather dark room.

For another hour, they sang. Both choirs took turns leading and each song was led by different singers. Everyone was given their moment to shine. This was a big moment to them. The pastor declared, "We have never had missionaries here before." Red was caught off guard, "Me a missionary? No way! I came seeking not to give!" To them, they did not care if those sent from God were officially appointed as missionaries or not. Their time of officially welcoming missionaries had come.

Gene was driving with ferocious aggression. Ma screamed, "Slow down!" Gene yelled back, "I can't! They have a half-hour lead on us. We have to make it up." Gus whined, "We don't even know where they went. They could have gone to another village or something." "Maybe they are headed back, we can't let them find their way back ahead of us." Just then, a huge pothole unfolded itself into the road. They were cruising exceedingly fast to stop. None of the passengers were wearing seatbelts for they were proving their toughness. In one quick motion, all were thrust upwards. Three distinct thumps were heard, "thunk, thunk, thunk" as their heads attempted to crush the ceiling. "That was the worst one yet!" A few stars were flickering in their eyes and eagerly roamed any which way. No one dared to scream or express any pain. Still, they kept the seatbelts off to prove something important to themselves.

They resumed their favorite pastime. Ma exclaimed, "You are the worst driver I have ever met!" Gus whipped in some sarcasm, "If there is just one little hole on the road, you always find it." Gene retorted, "I would like to see you do better!" Gus confidently replied, "Me, too, but wait, I am never given the chance to drive. You are just afraid that I will prove that I drive better than you." Gene attacked back even harder, "You have never proven yourself better than me in anything." Gus bullishly declared, "your memory is so short it is even non-existent. Do you remember how we started this trip? We were not even out of shade distance from a tree when you blared like a vacuum cleaner, "I will stay here with Ma while you go get the car!" Gene retorted, "I was taking care of ma." Gus attempted to draw some blood, "That was the first time you ever handed me the keys to drive. Very strange circumstances." Ma ridicules, "Your driving skills are so bad, I am surprised that you did not even call to ask us how to crank the vehicle." Gene chose an easier prey, "Ma, you say we are the worst drivers ever, did you not forget that you taught us to drive?" Gus rallied in, "Ma, according to your own words, you are the most extremely incompetent teacher ever twice over." At that moment, the driver hit a pothole hard just to prove a point. Ma ducked her head and curled her body as she slammed into the dash. In the very next moment, she was sucked into the floorboard. Gene prodded, "What are you doing down there? Taking a nap?" From below squealed, "Give me the keys right now." The other two were laughing so hard while Ma was staring up at them. Gus, in the back seat, raised his hands in slow motion and rolled over her seat as far as he could. He blared, "Slurp!" and disappeared under his seat except for his eyes so that he could see Ma's reaction. Gene also shrank down in his seat while driving, "Somebody help me! I'm drowning in the floorboard."

At the end of the service, they invited Sabrina to the front so that she may ask them questions. The pastor asked, "What is it that you wish to know?" Sabrina answered, "I would like to know how Christianity spread so fast in Africa?"

One man spoke up,

> "My dad told our whole village about Jesus! Nobody had ever heard that name before. My dad had only been a Christian for one day. He knew so little about God. He had heard one sermon and that was it. He went home and told his family. His dad, my grandpa, became very angry and told my dad to leave and never return. I can't imagine hearing these words. Grandpa said, 'Leave! Don't ever come back! You are no longer my son. Leave!' His dad pointed straight at him and at the gate. The finger kept pointing at my dad then at the gate."

The man stopped talking. Sabrina said, "You said that your father brought the Gospel to the village." The lady next to the man spoke up for the first time,

"Our father did bring the Gospel to the village. Dad left, and he came back with other Christians, and everyone listened. After they listened, they believed. Today, many, many, many believe because dad heard the Gospel and his heart beat for his family, his friends, his village."

Another woman spoke up, "Because dad was courageous, others chose to be courageous like him, and the Gospel spread to other villages around." Sabrina was astounded, "What kind of training did they get to tell others about Jesus?" The three siblings responded, "No training at all!" "They were left immediately!"

Another lady raised her voice, "The village down the road did not have a church! Somebody had to tell them about Jesus! So, we walked all night to tell them." Sabrina interrupted, "Who is we?" Another man spoke up, "The whole church walked." "Another still added in, "Women, men kids, everyone walked." "We walked all night and into the morning." "We told them all about Jesus." "We walked around all day talking to anyone who would listen." "When we were done in the evening, we still had to walk home all night and into the morning." Mickey had slipped through everyone to stand right by his mom. At that moment, he was really proud of his mom, and he let out a whisper that all could hear, "Yeah!" Everyone burst out laughing.

Back at home, Amy tossed on her bed. She rolled over and looked at the clock; it was 3 am. She moaned, "I wish I could sleep. I sure hope Pa is having fun. A little bit of growl seized her voice, "And that boy better get out of my head!"

Sabrina asked, "What made the new believers so eager to spread the Gospel?" The two continued, "The first believers were told that we became God's hands and feet." "We were God's ambassadors immediately." "It did not matter that we were trying to understand what Salvation meant, we were called as God's appointed to our friends, our family" "our country." The two laughed, "We were called to great service, even upon hearing the Gospel." With laughter in their voices, "We did not understand, but we were challenged to take up the best mission of all." "We knew we were being appointed by God to great service even as we were understanding Salvation." "We believed it could cost us everything." "It did!" "Dad rejected us until he grew old!" "We lost our jobs, our homes, our friends." "We did not know how we were going to make it!" Sabrina asked, "Did you regret risking it all." "Not for a second." Sabrina asked, "Why did you not regret it?" "Our hearts beat for God." "The real preacher was not the missionary." Together, "It was God Himself who spoke." "We knew that the missionary was telling the truth because God told us so!" "Our hearts were pounding so hard!" "We knew that we had come to the most important moment of our lives." "God shook us so hard." "Our maker made us feel so important" "so alive!" "Yes, so alive!"

Back inside blue was the rottenness of death. Ma turned to face Gene. She was pounding him with both fists at the same time. She elevated in unison her two clenched hands and drove them downwards with all her might into Gene's shoulder. She raised them again, and again and again, for she was trying her best to inflict much pain on her eldest son. Gus was in the backseat grinning until ma turned to look at him, then his face blanked until she turned away again to strike Gene. As quickly as they had left, the two invisible hooks latched onto the corners of the mouth and pulled up a smile with exceeding might.

Sabrina asked, "What was the last part of the sermon?" The two old men looked at each other then they spoke in unison, "We were told how to be saved." Sabrina asked dumbfoundedly, "Are you sure that how to be saved came at the end of the sermon?" They just looked at her and smiled. Sabrina echoed the reality, "You mean the missionary told you all about your calling before he told you the message of Salvation!?"

Sabrina turned to the two sisters and the brother who had told about their father going back to the village to tell his family about Jesus. "Is your father still living?" "No, he died a few years back." "What role does that make you have?" "We, are the keepers of the challenge!" Sabrina probed, "What is the challenge exactly?" "Run with God." "Run with all your might!" "He makes you feel so alive," "and so important." "Let His heartbeat in your life" "with such power." They quit talking, but it was obvious they were not finished. Sabrina had to know what they were not saying, "Just what?" "Just don't count the cost." "Any price is not enough!" Sabrina dug a little deeper, "What happens when someone says, 'I can't do that God, you are being unfair?'" "That special feeling of God's wonderful power leaves." "That's right! Life feels cold and heavy when we choose not to be God's hands and feet." "And, yeah!" "God's heart grows silent within!" Sabrina finished, "The heartbeat of missions!"

The pastor spoke to her again, many of us came from a long distance because we heard that you were looking for our missionaries. Some came to tell you stories; others are like you and long to hear."

Sabrina expressed herself, "Their leaving must have been a special moment." One spoke up, "He did come by our church one last time.

Zach was on his bed, but not exactly resting. His head and shoulders were in the middle of the bed. His back was bowed to the point where his knees were almost touching his head. He was folded in half where his feet were dangling above the pillows. All of a sudden, he forced his feet upwards. His body straightened so that his feet were almost scraping the ceiling and he was balanced on his shoulders. His neck was so bent it appeared broken. He let his feet fall. His body rocked and spun until his feet hit the floor and he was sitting on the edge of the bed. He looked at the clock, it is 4:30. He grumbled, "I don't get the value of falling in love. I neither get the girl nor can I sleep."

Somebody asked, "What did our pastor say?" Another spoke, "What were his last words?" "Remember, everyone in the room had risked their lives and their futures by telling their families about Christ." The eagerness to hear the final words caused the story to be interrupted. "He told us not to be half-Christians by telling only those we love about Christ. He told us to win the country for Christ. A full Christian's heart is one that burns for all people. He told us to be full Christians."

Sabrina asked, "Is there anything else about the missionaries?" A man stood up and walked over to the wall. He removed a picture and showed it to Sabrina. Our missionary had performed a large part of the ceremony of the wedding between the children of the presidents of our country and the neighboring country.

The next day, Amy arose and declared, "I am so tired, but the worst part is over. This craving for a stranger will start to fade. It always does ... I hope it does soooon."

Zach moaned while he lay on his stomach, "Oh, I got to get up. This is a terrible way to live. I must have messed up more with her than I thought." One leg slid out of the covers and onto the floor. "I had way too much energy when I was attempting to sleep. Now that I want to get up, I have no energy. Anyway, I need to move on from thinking about her. Craving what you don't have is not good."

A woman spoke to Sabrina, "We know you came to hear about the missionaries, but the pastor of our church has a story you will want to hear. Sabrina turned to the pastor and asked, "Will you please tell me your story?"

> "When I was a young man, I was very proud and was afraid of no one. A man was talking rudely to me. He thought he was someone great and could talk to me any way he so desired. He would not shut up so I beat him up good. The man told me that within six months, I would be dead. I laughed at him. Day after day came and nothing happened

to me. At the end of the six months, I saw a mist headed my way, I knew it was a very powerful curse. I tried to move around the approaching haze, but there was no place to go. The midst fell upon me. I became ill very quickly from the fog. I fell on my bed and lay there for three days. Each day, it was harder and harder to move. After a little bit, I could no longer move my arms or feet. As time passed, moving my fingers and toes became even more difficult. Eventually, I could no longer move my extremities. All I could do was lay there and breathe. Even the simple act of respiration grew into a labored chore. By the end of the third day, I could not breathe enough to live much longer. I knew I was about to die, so in desperation, I called out, 'Jesus, Jesus, save me!' That man who put that curse on me was a powerful witch doctor. I knew better than to beat him up, but I was proud. Jesus saved me."

Sabrina pondered, what kind of crazy man am I interviewing? Another man who was sitting there knew her skepticism. He declared, "This man is the pastor of a very large church. He is highly respected not only in his church but all over the country."

CHAPTER 11
FOUND

The crooks were sitting in their blue car in the shade of a mango tree. Ma declared, "You are going to have to let me out again. We have sat here so long; I have to pee again." When the van passed. Ma was opening the car door. She was twisting her body to get out. Gene reached up to the key and cranked the car. Ma had two feet on the ground. Gene shifted the car in D and began to roll slowly. Ma snapped, "You are not going to leave me behind again. I will not stand for it! Enough is enough!" Gene said, "We have company, it is time to go!" Ma declared, "But, I got to go!" In a very rare caring moment, Gene stated, "I know, Ma, but we have company. We gotta go."

Sabrina asked her son, "So what did you really like about the trip to Africa?" "I just like how God moved through them with such great power." "It is something I thought I would never see." The ladies spoke up, "I had a favorite part, too. I had always thought that being safe was the most important part, but they risked a lot." "Yeah, I was thinking the same thing. Their heartbeat was for the people and not to be safe." "Safe is important, too!" "Oh, yes, yes, most definitely."

Ma claimed, "This trip is going to be a success after all." Gus uttered in amazement, "We just about have the impossible in our hands." Gene declared, "Why don't you just admit it? I was pretty amazing. Just admit it!" Gus conceded, "You were right, going to Africa to chase down teleportation was a good call, but we don't have the ability yet. Don't let your head get too big." "I have done what no other crook has ever done, I have discovered teleportation."

Mickey's aunt and grandmother weighed in on what they thought was most important. "I always thought that above all else I had to be safe." "Oh, that is right, if you are not safe, then you risk losing everything." "Being safe is very important, but we came to see a people who chose not to be safe." "In choosing to lose it all, they found life." "They to live by trusting God with all."

Ma, "You have got to stop. I got to pee!" Gene handed her a bottle. Ma exclaimed, "What are you giving me that bottle for? You know women can pee in a bottle, but women need their privacy." She shoved the bottle back at him. He then set the bottle back right in front of her, "I don't see a problem, prove yourself that women can pee in a bottle!" A stunned look smeared across her face. "You, you, you don't think I am a woman?" Gus was laughing so hard from the back seat, "Oh, this is too good to be true." Ma turned and stared at Gus. "Y'all don't think I am a woman? I am your Ma! Where do you think you came from? Eggs?"

Ma yelled, "You have got to stop this car right now! I am going to leak all over the place." Gene responded seriously, "But Ma, we will lose them again!" Ma retorted, "With your driving, we will catch them in no time flat!" Gene removed his foot from the accelerator and began to brake.

Out in the middle of nowhere, the blue car was parked by the side of the jungle. Gene was sitting on the horn. He had really taken the expression to a new level. He had twisted his amply oversized body somehow which enabled him to sit on the horn. Every now and then, he pulled up just enough for the blaring to stop, he then sat back down on it. As much as Ma longed to run to hurry, she took her time when she appeared out of the bushes; after all, it was a matter of war with her son. Gene snapped, "If the turtle was racing you, he would have won." "You amaze me, I did not know a walrus could sit on a horn."

CHAPTER 12
LOST LOVE

Amy had not been in town since her encounter with her three least favorites from high school. She conducted slowly toward the diner where she liked to splurge on an ice-cream float on a hot day, "A double ice-cream cone would be perfect today." She peered into the diner and saw the three. "Then again, who needs ice-cream anyway?" She drove off to avoid contact. A few blocks later, she slipped between two yellow lines, and disengaged the transmission. She emitted herself from the car and stalled just a moment before entering. "That was too close!" She released a sigh of relief. She regained her composure and stood really tall, then entered Party Parts. She immediately went over to a display and unhooked a package of balloons. She turned the corner, and nearly bumped into a man standing there. She softly stated, "Excuse me!" The man turned around and it was Zach. She released out a brief, "Oh!" Zach stampeded out a peppy, "Oh!" As much as she wished to be guarded, she could not resist a smile.

She asked, "Who are you here getting party favors for?" Zach started to answer; his mouth opened. He kept it open, and without saying anything, he cocked his head slightly. His mom was putting on a baby shower for a friend, and he was in charge of decorations. The job of decorating again for his mother was not one he liked, but it brought her much satisfaction for her son to be a part of her life. He finally answered with a very pleased, and high pitched, "Hmm!" Amy was at a loss for words thinking that Zach did not wish for her to come. Her emotions shocked her, she felt left out as if the love of her life had moved on! Her fantasy world crushed in that moment. She thought she could play hard-to-get and when she was finally ready if that time ever came, she would let the guy in slowly.

The little spot in the store became very crowded. Amy was really close, but had not stepped back yet for she was uncomfortable with the distance she felt from him; yet with the little space three bodies still found room between him and her. They didn't just get close, but all three were touching him at the same time. One was leaning into him like it was her spot – her comfort zone. Another had arm draped on his right shoulder with her hand curled around his neck, and the fingers stretched all the way to his cheek. The last had established a parking zone for her hand on his chest. "I have missed our daily chats since high school!" "We had an amazing time!" "Those were the best of days!" Amy sought to bolt out the door, but that would have been declaring defeat. The trio played their game perfectly. To Zach, they continued their sweet nothings, "I've been wondering, how have you been?" "I miss those days so much!" "You were the smartest guy in the high school!" They made sure to keep his full attention while one by one they turned to Amy and charmingly whispered hate, "You thought you could run away and hide, but we saw you drive off." "If you are wanting to catch a real man, let us show you how to do it!" "He is ours anytime we choose to claim him."

Zach was in an awkward spot. His heart was burning for Amy, but she was doing her best to put the fire out so it seemed. Zach's mind wandered back to math class. Those three were in his class every year. Many guys tried to hang around the three lovely prizes. Zach knew the rules of the game. They would flirt, laugh, and gently touched him every day. All he had to do was help them in math during class, and never show any romantic interest. The game was good for all. He made sure he learned the math lesson before class, so he could help them in math even if they really didn't need it. The charade was a massive success. The gals needed to display how adorably charming they were. The sweeter they were to Zach, the more the other guys fought for their attention. In return, Zach was a lot more popular; besides, the game was fun – real fun.

On this particular day, Zach knew that their attention probably had more to do with Amy than him. He didn't care – well, he did care – but his concerns were different than Amy's. They were friends, and they were always loyal. Today, they were giving him a gift. They were turning the shunned one into the center piece. Amy walked away at a browsing speed. She found the items she was looking for and headed for the register. The whole time, she heard the chatter and laughter from the gals, and occasionally the rumble of his voice. Her fantasy world of protecting herself from the dangers of boys had fallen into the shredder, and the endless tatters laid sprayed all over the floor mocking her. She wondered how things could get any worse while not knowing that tomorrow was going to be a lot worse for trouble far greater than drama was on a conquest.

Up ahead of the van, the traffic was moving slowly because of construction. They moved along at what seemed to be a crawl speed, but they did not stop as they passed the workers. Sabrina declared triumphantly, "That was not so bad!" The vehicles returned to normal speed.

Gene was so proud of himself. He kept saying as he roared by another car trying to catch up, "Ma, watch this!" "I got another one!" "No problem!" "Sucker!" "It's no biggie! We will catch them in no time!" All of a sudden, in the middle of the road, was a large truck just parked. He slammed on his brakes. He could not stop in time, so he veered into the oncoming lane. Ma responded, "I'm watching and you nearly got us killed!" Gene let out, "Aw, no!" Ma snorted, "What?" "Construction! We are stuck!" Ma prompted, "Isn't there any way around this?" "We are in the middle of the jungle." The mood was heavy, and no one felt like fighting.

Amy was setting decorations around the house to welcome back pa. "I can't believe my three worst enemies took my beau away." She realized what she just confessed to herself! "Well, he could have been my man had I wanted one! There has to be something seriously wrong with him to hang around trash like that. Every time I say, 'This is the worst possible thing they could do to me – there is no way they could ever be meaner!' They always find a way to blast me with a new level of hate."

Zach emitted a chuckle. "That was good! That was really good. My three amigas have always looked out after me. To have the three most popular cuties fight over me in front of a girl playing hard to get, it just doesn't get any better than that."

CHAPTER 13
FRUIT BATS

The mother and daughter think-a-likes declared, "Stop at that park!" "This is a great place to stop!" "We have a few minutes until the sun sets." "Let's stretch our legs!" "We could use a little exercise after sitting in a cramped car all day!" Red and Mickey looked at each other. They had been taking turns in the back of the van all day. They both felt beaten up, but neither had said a word. They walked the park along the beach. Huge ten-foot waves crashed the beach just offshore. The two continued, "I have never seen such large waves in all my life." "I have seen them on TV, but not in real life." "Such magnificent waves." "They sure are!"

Mother and daughter were quite talkative as usual. "Look at the little birds up in the sky." "They can't be that big, but they are way up there." Red just grinned and looked away. Every time that his aunt and grandmother went to talk, Mickey was super curious about what Red thought about the two. Mickey rushed over to Red. "You laughed! What is so funny?" "Those are not little birds up in the sky. Well, the bodies are little like that of a dove, but the wingspan is three feet." "No way! What kind of bird has a super little body and massive wings?" "Bats!" "Bats? Vampires?" "No, fruit bats called straw-colored fruit bats! They eat fruit!" Red halted a moment before switching to his biggest Dracula voice, "And they don't drink blooood! Ha! Ha! Ha! Ha!"

Ma said, "What now genius?" "You know my name is not Gene, and definitely not Genius." "I know, but right now, I am hoping you live up to the name of Genius!" "I can't find them." "But you have a plan!" "How are you supposed to find five people in a city of six million officially, but the unofficial guess is more like sixteen million in one night?" Gus had been silent the whole trip back, "Seriously, what is your plan?" "I got it! I figured out what we should do next!" The other two said in an excited tone, "What is that?" Gene replied, "Let's go eat!" Both were delighted! "OOOoooh!" I know a park where we can watch the traffic flow to the airport. There is a plane leaving for the States before long. If they were leaving tonight, we should be able to see them pass by."

Sabrina compares, "The waves are so full of energy! They are like a toddler that keeps going, except these waves never sleep!" Mickey replied, "Mom, you are always saying something like that!" Red stated, "The wave has a much bigger temper tantrum than toddlers. Caught in one of those waves could be difficult. Sabrina smiled. Mickey smarted off, "Difficult? Difficult? Out of all the words you could have chosen, like 'disastrous,' or 'terrible,' 'awful,' tragic, 'devastating', 'calamitous' …" "Calamitous? Impressive using words like that!" Mickey blushes which pleased his mother.

Unmasked, but gloved were two ladies carrying a cut open baguette with chunks of meat in it. Mickey asked, "Why do you need gloves if you are going to inhale the food?" "So, our hands don't get dirty." "When you finish eating, you are going to take off the gloves and wash your hands anyway." Both of the women shook their heads, "You just don't understand." "Anyway, this is the most amazing meal I have ever had." "That is right! I have never tasted chicken so sweet in my life!" "By far, the best chicken ever!" "Oh, I agree!" "What did they do? Feed the chicken sugar or what?" "Whatever they did, they will make a fortune selling it around the world!"

Red let them gush over the food before telling them the truth. "They did feed the birds nothing but sugar!" Mickey and Sabrina gazed at Red fully puzzled. "The birds eat nothing but sugar in the form of fruit. Nothing but fruit!" All of a sudden, Mickey understood. His hands rushed up to cover his face. He bent over, and jumped up and down. In astonishment, he blurted a "Oh, ho, ho, ho!" The three ladies looked at him like he went crazy. Still clueless, the munchers declared, "It is really, really good!" "You should try some!" At that moment, they both took a large bite of baguette filled with meat to display what the others were missing. They ended up tearing off a bite with a piece of "chicken" that was dangling out of their mouths so with a gloved hand they pushed the morsel inside. "Humh! They declared.

Mickey was ready to steal their fun! "That meat is not chicken!" Together they both emitted a half garbled, "What is it then?" Mickey and Red looked at each both and were wishing to say it in unison. They look back at the women. By then, they had quit chewing, but their mouths were not closed because it is so full food. The guys stared at the mother / daughter. With great joy, they pointed upwards. The women looked at those tiny little birds in the sky. They heard a muffled, "Chickens don't fly that high." "What flies that high?" They knew that they were going to dread the answer, but they had to know. Together, "What is it?" Likewise, the fellas boomed in unison, "Bats, fruit bats!" All of a sudden, the food was not nearly so good. They threw down their baguettes; they spit out their mouthfuls; they gaged just as hard as their bodies permitted. The other three thundered belly laughs.

Gene drove across town and pulled into a park by the beach. "Why did you choose this park?" asked Gus. "It is a great place to eat." "You wouldn't know. You have never eaten here before." "It is on the road to the airport." "Humh! They have to pass by!" "Precisely!" Ma snorted in, "You mean you plan on living here until they go to the airport? That is ridiculous!" "Think before you judge! They headed back to the capital probably to catch a plane either tonight or in the morning." "So that means we are spending all night here?" "Think some more! The plane they would most likely catch tonight leaves in a few hours, so they will be passing by shortly if they come tonight." "And if they don't! If you weren't so judgmental, I would have told you the whole plan. We will find them."

Amy was sound asleep. She was hugging her pillow. All of a sudden, she was wide awake. She sat up, still with her feet on the bed. "Oh, no! No, no, no, no no! Pa is in trouble! Big trouble! I feel it!" She looked at the clock – it is two a.m."

Zach was sprawled all over the bed. In a snap, he woke up. "Oh, no! No, no, no, no no! Amy is in trouble. I can feel it." He hopped up on his hands and knees and stared at the clock which also said two a.m.

Amy slid off the edge of the bed and dropped to her knees. She propped her elbows on the bed. Her palms were sealed together, and her thumbs were gently pressed against her nose. "Oh, Lord! Protect Pa! I don't know what is going on, but You do. Oh, God! Please protect Pa! Send your angels to guard him!"

Zach slid off his bed as well, but to the other side. He planted his knees firmly into the floor. His elbows were further apart, his palms were resting near his temples, and he prayed, "God, I don't know what trouble Amy has found, but she needs Your peace. Wrap her in Your mercy, Your kindness, and Your love."

Amy arose to find her phone, "He hasn't contacted me yet. He does not have service unless he is at a hotel and uses Wi-Fi. He has no way to contact for help. What should I do? What should I do?"

Zach stood up and searched for his phone. He knocked it on the floor. He picked it up. "No messages!"

Amy pondered, "I could call Zach! At two a.m.? And tell him what? I had a feeling that Pa is in trouble."

Zach verbalized, "I could call Amy, and ask her what is going on? I would wake her up and she would say, 'I was asleep! What do you mean what is going on?' I would ruin things for sure then."

Amy decides, "Call Zach? No way!"

Zach resolves, "Call Amy? Not on my life!"

Amy crawled back in bed and stared at the ceiling!

Likewise, Zach lunged upward and plummeted onto his back. He unfolded his limbs and laid on his back.

At the beach, Red was standing in the walkway with his back turned. The sun was setting making identifying people all that much harder. Ma was headed straight for Red. She turned on her walkie-talkie and wedged the buds into her ears. As she came upon Red, close enough to bump into him, she heard the crackling of a voice, "I see their van!" She turned around and stared toward the lit highway. The voice continued, "Never mind, it was not them. Ma continued to walk as she turned around. She bumped straight into Red and muttered, "Pardon!" Although the word is the same in both English and French, her version sounded very American. Pa was staring at his phone just wishing he could contact Amy. Lost in his thoughts, he neither made an attempt to answer her nor realized who she was. The lady continued past him.

Amy slid back to her knees. "God, I feel the crisis has passed by thank you for protecting Pa!"

Zach said, "Oh!" as if relief had come! Zach moved to the praying position; except, it was upside down. In an innocent, upside down as only a youngster would do. He slid off the bed head first until his elbows reached the floor. He brought his hands together directly in front of his face. He bent at the hips so that only his knees would touch the bed and cocked his feet back as close to his derriere as possible. He spoke to his Maker again, "Thank you that whatever happened, you spared Amy!"

CHAPTER 14
CONDITIONER

At the hotel, Red was unpacking the van from the hatch. Mickey was pulling things out from crannies and was setting the stuff by the van. Approaching the van, the bat-eaters gripped, "That is the most disgusting thing in all my life." "I could live four lifetimes and never eat anything as disgusting as bats." "Oh, that is a conservative number. You may never even hear of eating anything as disgusting as bats, much less consume it." Red interjected, "One thing you two are right about, an appropriate time comes to be cautious." "See, eating the bats did have an effect on him." "I am very surprised; you could be more cautious." Red squeezes his lips tight to keep from laughing. "Could I have a pair of gloves? I need to be more cautious." "A pair of gloves? Sure, here you go!" A pair of gloves was offered to him. The grandmother pulls a pair of gloves out of a bag. "Don't just take one pair, you might feel like you need another." "Thank you! Thank you! I am very sure that I will need both." He grabbed the second pair as well. "Would it be an inconvenience if I kept the bag as well?" "Absolutely not. We have many more. You can have as many as you like." "This is perfect just the way it is."

Red was sitting in a hotel room all by himself. He peeked into his butterfly cage. The floor of the cage was littered with immobile butterflies. "Strange how many butterflies have died. It is ... no! It can't be! It is like they just died on purpose."

Red grabbed a pair of gloves. He turned them over and stared at them. "Will they work? Can the gloves keep the dead butterflies from vaporizing upon touch?" He donned on both gloves, then he just waited trying to get up the nerve. He kept one hand over the entrance of the cage to avoid any butterflies from escaping. With the other hand, he poked one dead butterfly. Nothing happened. He poked it again. Still, nothing out of the ordinary happened. He grabbed one stiff butterfly and pulled it out. Meticulously, he snared the still beings one at a time and piled them on the desk. After a little bit, only the living remained behind the netting.

"Now what?" Red walked around the room looking for something. "There is nothing to work with." After giving up on his search, he rested his backside up against the sink. Red became a little high-strung. He started slapping the countertop with both hands behind him. In rapid succession, the thumping created a steady quick beat. He thrust out, "There has got be to something? His hands slung forward. One finger clipped the conditioner bottle and sling-shotted the mini-bottle to the floor. Immediately, Red picked it up, Sorry buddy. I didn't mean to throw you around like that." He stared at the bottle that said, "Conditioner." "Hey, that will do!"

He took the conditioner over to the desk. He opened the bag, with one big swoop, he brushed all the wings into the bag. Next, he squeezed the bag, then he stared at the broken butterfly wings. He rolled the bag between his palms for a little bit. He looked in the bag and saw small pieces of wings. He closed the bag anew, and spun the bag more viciously between his hands. After a little bit, he peeked inside, and noticed nothing but butterfly wing dust. "Exactly right!"

Red angled the bag of butterfly wings until one corner of the bag was the dust. The other corner up in the air was empty. He directed the empty bag tip between his eye teeth. He clamped his jaw shut, he pulled and twisted the bag. The bag stretched and eventually the smallest part of the corner ripped away. He pinched the corner, then spun the see-through container upside down. The black and yellow powder rested pinched above the hole. With the free hand, he lifted the conditioner bottle. He held the bottle between his pinkie and his palm. With the thumb and index fingers, he spun off the cap. The bottle was once again redirected to the table's surface. He guided the ripped corner directly above and then into the conditioner bottle. He removed a paperclip from his book, then he stretched it out until it is somewhat straight. He used it to stir the conditioner. He removed his stir stick that was covered with a grayish substance. "Humh, I can't let it go to waste." Just then the hotel phone rang. He answered, "Hey … Okay … I'll be right over!"

CHAPTER 15
THE OUT-OF-CONTROL EXPERIMENT

Red grabbed something from his bag, and walked out the door to the room across the hall. He reached up to knock. As he swung forward his knuckles to knock on the door, it opened. Mickey declared, "Come on in!" Red was amused by missing the door so he lets out a small chuckle, "Ahruh!" Red grabbed a seat on the bed. In the room already were the other four. The pair were laughing. "We definitely had chicken earlier!" "That is right; we sure did." Mickey interrupted, "No, it was not chicken!" "Young man, when we thought we were eating chicken, we were anything but chicken!" "When we realized we were eating bat, we became chicken!" Everyone laughed. "See, we had chicken earlier!"

Red was holding the paper clip between his index and thumb pointed backwards so that no one could see what he was holding. He twisted his wrist so that only he could see the paperclip. With the thumb and index from the other hand, he pinched the metal pole, and pulled it out. All the conditioner with the butterfly wing's mixture from the stir end was wiped clean off. He rubbed his thumb and index together. He muttered to himself, "We will see if it works." His hand slid into his pocket and removed a pencil flashlight. He turned on the light so that still no one could see what he was doing. The finger slipped across the end of the flashlight. All of a sudden, everything stopped.

Red rose and walked over to Mickey. He tapped on the boy, "Humh, hard as stone!" All the adults were wearing glasses. He removed one lady's glasses, and walked over to another. Likewise, he took her glasses, and put on the pair from the other lady. He tried to swap glasses, himself, but the frames were too narrow. He rushed back to Sabrina, and switched glasses once again. This pair had flexible arms. Red muttered, "What an amazing lady!" He reached down and grabbed Sabrina's ankle and lifted. He rocked her backwards, but no part of her bent. He removed her shoes. One by one he took off everyone's shoes and swapped them around. He was left with a pair for himself, no matter how he tried, he could not slide his foot in. He left Mickey's shoes on. He untied the shoe string laces, then he re-tied them so that the feet were stuck together.

Red flowed across the room until he faced Sabrina. He lifted her foot ever so slightly. He pulled off her shoe and threw on her another. He proceeded to do the same with other foot. He sat her foot back on the ground. The plan seemed to work for a moment. It was almost not noticeable at first, but she started to move. She fell over on the bed, then she continued to rock forward. "Oh no you don't!" commanded Red. He grabbed her to keep her from falling. He tried to sit her back up again, but every attempt failed. She kept inching over to fall. He held her up and stretched to grab a pillow. He tilted her enough the other way, to slide the pillow under her on one side. He released, but his hand stayed close. Before long she resumed her plummet the other way. He tried readjusting her three or four times by repositioning the pillow. It did not work. He would have settled her in a chair, but the two were occupied.

He laid her down in bed. "Eeeh! Too romantic. If she ever found out it was me, laying her down in bed that would be so inappropriate. This can't be happening to me. There is only one place I can put her, and it is inappropriate, too." He picked her up and carried her to the only other room – the restroom. He sat her down by placing the feet on the floor. He then angled her backwards to let her down, then commanded, "Wait! Wait! Wait! Wait!" He saw that her seat had a hole in it. He knew she couldn't hear him, but he talked to her just the same. He angled her forward enough for clearance. He spun the lid downward, but it caught on her hindermost parts, and the cover came to a complete stop. "I did not mean to spank you. Although, you do have a heart hard like stone right this moment. I never thought I would say that about you." He lifted her further, and the lid cleared. He sat her down, "There, all is good!" He let go, and she proved herself to still be unsteady. He looked at her feet, and one was slightly higher than the other. He reached for the towel like bath mat. He wadded it up enough under one foot and she finally stayed! "Voilà!" He returned into the other room, and said, "I can't move just one woman, and her to the toilet. They all have to be moved in extreme ways."

Red looked around the room. He pulled the chairs around the quarters so that the people were seated in different spots. Another idea zapped him. He lifted grandmother's chair and placed it on the table.

He picked up Mickey. The man spun the boy upside down and placed him by the window. This window was a very typical tropical window with a crank arm to open and close it. He wrapped the tied shoe laces around the mechanical arm. Red let the boy's head and shoulders down on the floor, the rest of him was suspended in air by the laces.

The other gloved woman was stationed in the second chair. He attempted to lift her. He struggled for this woman had accumulated a lot more size than her mother. You will really freak out if your chair is in the middle of the bed." Red backed the chair all the way against the bed. "I'll get it this time." Red lifted with all his strength. The chair rose about six inches off the ground, then the lady surprisingly started a slow slide in her chair. Red screamed, "No, no, no, no, no!" The female completely slipped off the seat. He tried to stop her, but she was just too much woman for him. Red fell over backwards; she continued her forward progression. Gravity carried her until she pinned Red directly underneath her. Red blurted, "If I ever desired to be trapped by a woman, it would not be you." Her stiffness kept her from falling all the way upon him.

Red thought out loud, "What do I do? This is definitely terrible. This is way more ... Please, please don't wake up until I figure something out." At that moment, time started again. The woman collapsed directly upon him. For a moment, he disappeared. She screamed with all her might. Red was trying to hold her off, but he was not strong enough. She dropped forward the last five inches until her lips met his, and they were staring each other down eyeball to eyeball. A blood curling scream erupted from her. She was hyperventilating as she yelled. She was extremely frightened, and he was equally terrified. In return, he screamed as well.

When Sabrina woke up, she heard four people screaming from the other room. Her first encounter was the two on the floor. She reached down to them, but then she heard her mother scream. She rushed over to the table, but stopped and stared in disbelief. She heard her son call out, "Mom, help me! I'm stuck." He was trying to wiggle free, but he remained half-suspended in air. She left her mother on the table. She darted over to her son. She tried to untangle the shoes strings, but they were pulled tight by her son's weight. She grabbed the heel of his shoe and ripped it off of him. Very quickly, she freed the other foot as well.

The woman, who loomed over the man, screamed! Stopped! A puzzled look fell over her face; then in a feeling of triumph, she smiled! The thought of Red trapped beneath her thrilled her. She realized that fate had dumped a man into her lap so she was not about to let him go quickly. Her grin elicited new emotions from Red. He saw himself being so controlled by her manias that he was in an isolation suit, and she declared, "Don't you feel better."

The next scene, he visualized himself at the altar, with plastic gloves and a face mask, then she pulled him in closer for the kiss. That scene was enough. Red declared his independence; he put his foot to the side for leverage and pushed. She rolled to the side. As soon as freed from the weight, Red rolled back the other way. He jumped up to help grandmother off the table.

By the rescue, grandmother was sitting calmly in her seat just laughing at the incident on the floor. Sabrina zoomed over to the next crisis, and she positioned her hands opposite Red's on the chair. One hand gripped the back of the chair, the other locked on the armrest. Quickly, they lifted grandmother who seemed to be enjoying the ride.

A mélange of phrases erupted from everyone. "How can you see with these glasses?" "You must be totally bind?" "These glasses give me a headache." "These shoes are so big; they are like a tank." "How can anyone keep their balance with feet this small?" "This is not my color!" "I can't believe anyone would wear this style!" Red did not know how to enter into the conversation. He sure did not want to let it slip that he was not in shock over the event; but then again, he never dreamed he would eagerly have put himself in a nightmare.

Before long, a more serious dialogue took precedent, "What happened to us anyway?" "I don't know!" "Could it happen again?" "Is this world as we know it falling apart?" While the gals were so serious, Mickey was laughing so hard. "That was so cool! It was like we teleported or something!" As soon as he opened his mouth, he knew that he had said too much. He quickly glanced at Red, who said nothing, then he stared at his mom. The twinish responded like it was the most absurd idea. "Teleporting? Where in the world would you get that idea?" "That is the strangest way to describe this that I could imagine." His mom said nothing about it, but she knew that her son had more to say – later! Quickly she changed the subject. "Why don't you see if anything has gone missing?" "Oh my, my money!" "The gloves and masks!" Quickly the two women sped out to attack their belongings. Red quickly saw an opportunity to escape. "Oh, my stuff!" He existed without giving Sabrina a chance to ask questions.

Left in the room were mother and son. Sabrina commanded, "You had better start talking!" Mickey explained, "I really don't know what happened. I never dreamed something like what just happened could be a

> reality." "I am sure you are not lying, nor are you telling me everything you know!" "I am not lying! You know that field where Red and I hunted butterflies. That field is a historical field for teleportation. There are recorded stories throughout history of people teleporting during thunderstorms. Some very dangerous people were there trying to figure out how the teleportation worked. They assumed that because Red and I were out there, we knew something. So, they threatened us, and they were going to hurt me."

Sabrina asked, "And you did not think this was something to tell me?" "How Mom? Some people are going to hurt us if we don't explain how to teleport? You have asked so many questions that I would have felt so dumb." Sabrina realized that her son was scared. "I do ask too many questions. When my curiosity drives me on, I keep asking the same question in a different manner." "Yeah, you do Mom, and you drive me crazy. I don't try to keep information back – I just don't know to say it." "It won't happen again!" "Okay! Thanks, Mom!" "Sorry!" Mickey hugged his mom!

After a thorough hug, Sabrina, all of a sudden, pushed her son far enough back so she could look at his face. "I won't torture you, but you are not finished either." "How did you get away?" "They let us go to give Red time to ask the natives, and to figure it out. You drove up and we fled. We seemed to have escaped them." "Did Red do … teleport the items tonight?" "I don't know. I really don't. He wouldn't tell me if he did. He has figured out how to teleport because I saw him jump from one place to another, but he did not jump far. He was not very good at it." "So, what else happened?" "Nothing!" "What is Red's plan about dealing with the terrible people? About teleportation?" With a huge slur in his voice, "Mom!" "Sorry Son, I did it again." She leaned over and kissed him on the forehead near the temple.

Red rushed into his bedroom. He ran and jumped onto the bed landing on his back. "I sure made a mess of things tonight. Now, they all know this teleporting / time stopping stuff is real. "Okay, Okay, God I get it!" Red slid off his bed, to his knees and prayed, "Dear God, I made a mess of things tonight. I thought I would use the power to be funny. Now I see that great power is sacred, and holy, to be honored and revered. I give you this mess for You to fix!" Red paused then belched a small chuckle. "You had a way of humbling me tonight, by letting that woman whose mannerisms are repulsive pin me to the ground."

Darkness had fallen over the beach. On the other side of the street, were thousands of little shacks all wedged together. Poor squatters covered the landside who had left their villages looking for a better life. Ma concluded, "We better not stay – it may not be safe!" Gene concurred, "You're right, Ma! If they have not gone to the airport yet, they are not going tonight." Gus wondered, "Do you think we will find them?" "We will find them! I just hope you are not sleepy." "Hunh?" "We will join them for breakfast!" Ma snapped, "How?"

Amy slid into the gas station. She was pumping her gas when a convertible pulled up on the other side of the island. The occupants were quick to start a conversation. "Well, hello Amy … Amy is your name, isn't it?" "Yes, that is her name!" "I wonder if Zach knows that's her name." "We saw you the other day drooling over him!" "Lots of slobber!" "Disgustinnng!" Amy said nothing to her three tormenters, but she didn't need to; her face was burning red. "Look at her glow!" "She must really like Zach!"

CHAPTER 16
CAUGHT

The blue car poked its way through the parking lot. "Nope, the van is not here, either!" "How many hotels have we been to now?" "That makes twelve!" They pulled out into the street. Gus was staring at his phone. "There is another hotel just down the block." They pull up, but a new problem sprung up. The hotel's parking lot was locked up behind a twenty-foot wall. Ma snapped, "How do you plan on inspecting that parking lot?" No answer pursued. Gene pulled up to the attendant at the gate. "Speak English?" "Non!" The attendant motioned for them to get out of the car. Gus grumped, "Great, even when we are in, we can't see the parking lot because it is valley parking." Gene gave orders, "I will check prices! Gus unloads the car very slowly. Ma, you slip off and get some exercise. We all know that you need it."

Gene entered the building. Gus started by picking up all the trash in the vehicle. He mumbled, "I just think this is Gene's way of getting someone else to clean the car. I know he won't come back until I finish cleaning the car." Ma headed toward the door to enter. Gene addressed the worker, "Do you have a trash bag?" The poor man did not understand. Gene flared his arms like getting a trash bag was so important. Ma quickly slipped away into the darkness for the porter had lost containment of the situation.

At three a.m., the phone rang. Sabrina called her mother, but she did not answer. "She must already be at breakfast, son. Are you ready?" "Almost!" Mickey was moving very slowly toward the bathroom as slumber fervently controlled his body.

Red strolled into the restaurant. He saw the mother daughter duo. Normally, Red would sit with them, but after last night, being pinned under a smiling face, he decided to find another table. Without a word, three shadows filled the remaining seats. "It is good seeing you this morning!" "We have been looking all over the place for you!" "Did you really think you could run away from us?" "You betrayed us!" "We let you go so that you could tell us how this teleportation thing works." Red stated the obvious, "We all know that teleportation is a myth!" "You would dare fib to us?"

The waiter toted food to the table for two. In came Sabrina and Mickey. She saw Red at a table with strangers. She started to head his way. Mickey grabbed her arm and tugged. Sabrina stopped and stared at her son. Their eyes locked for a few moments. Neither blinked nor flinched. Sabrina understood that the three had come to collect the powers of teleportation.

Sabrina changed direction, and marched toward her family with urgency. They both raised their heads upon completion of giving thanks. "I am sure hungry." "I am, too." "We did not get to eat much last night!" "That was disgusting – eating vampires!" "I'm starving!" In unison, they picked up their forks; scooped a bite and inserted. "This is really good!" "Excellent!"

Ma started with what she did best, "I would hate for those women to lose their minds and go swimming in the sea." Gene didn't want to miss out on the intimidation, "With the violence of the clapping of the waves, they would disappear in no time – never to be heard of again." Ma snapped her fingers, "Just like that and they're gone." Gene leaned forward until his face was inches away from Red. "You said, 'Teleportation does not exist!'" Gus spoke for the first time, "I saw you jump from one place to another. Cool trick! Still pathetic." "You could only jump about a yard at a time!" "You just don't yet have the touch. If you did, you would already be gone with all your friends here."

In a low firm voice, Sabrina commanded her sister and mother, "You are done eating. Let's go right now!" "But I'm hungry!" "And we have time!" They both reached down with their forks to retrieve another bite. With both hands, Sabrina reached out and jerked away their forks. "Shh! I said let's go! Now!" "Oh?!" For once, only one of the two spoke and the other did not join in. Sabrina started to lead them out away from Red. "What ..." "Shh!" They followed Sabrina and Mickey in silence.

Ma and Gene were seated so close to Red to pinning him in. Ma questioned, "Who are you?" Red said nothing. Ma and Gene reach into Reds pockets. Their fingers locked onto the contents. With closed claws, they extracted the contents of his pants. Gene said, "Look a flashlight! A bottle of ... of ... of conditioner!" Ma gloated on their newfound treasures. "A wallet and a phone." Gene concluded, "Maybe the teleportation power is hidden in the flashlight." Gene unscrewed the flashlight, and removed the batteries. "Not here! Maybe in the lens." He proceeded to disassemble the head of the torch. Red sadly watched as his plan for escape had been unscrewed.

As soon as the little band exited the door, Sabrina barked, "Let's go!" "We need to check the rooms." "Red insisted that everything was to be packed in the car last night. Let's go!" The protest grew firmer, "Our toothbrushes!" "Our gloves!" "Our masks!" "We can't go without them." "No, we can't!" "And we most definitely can't leave without Red!" Sabrina admitted, "We can't help Red. He is giving us time to escape." "Escape what?" Mickey meddled in the conversation for the first time, "Those three who plan on killing him." The two ladies spoke rashly, "We need to do something to help him." "That's right! We must save him." Mickey continued, "And us?" "Are you sure?" "We could fight armed bandits? Think about it!" "But what about Red?" Sabrina answered, "He is on his own." Mickey boasted, "Red will be okay. He will teleport out!" "Teleportation doesn't exist!" "It is just nonsense." Mickey questioned, "What do you think happened last night?" "Oh!" The one, who had been enchanted by waking up on Red, declared, "Ohhh! So Red dropped me on top of himself last night. Why that dirty little old man!" Mickey defended, "Red is just not that good at teleporting yet!" In a devastating moment, she expressed her disappointment by dropping from a top note to a very low note, "Oh!"

Ma opened Red's wallet and removed his driver's license. "1102 Willow Street, Hughville!" "Gene declared, now we know where you live. You can never run from us again." "We know who you are and where you live." Ma seized his phone. and turned it on. The locked screen blocked her. "Open it!" He just sat there. "We are letting your friends escape. Open your phone. We can catch them in the parking lot where no one is looking. Now open your phone. Ma yanked his thumb, and placed it on the scanner. The phone screen changed. "Perfect!" She tapped the picture icon. "Look who will we find! Aw! A pretty young girl. Another picture of her. And another. And another. They are nearly all of her. Why that adorable girl is your whole life?"

Gene interrupted, "What is her name?" Red still said nothing. "Why are you being so difficult? You don't want our attitude to be any worse toward you than it is already. Now talk!" Red still spoke nothing. Ma continued rambling, "Her name is easy to find. She closed the pictures and tapped the phone button. "Who have you called lately? The last one was to Amy! Amy! Amy! And Amy!" She looked at Gene, "What do you think his daughter's name is?" "I wonder if it is Amy." Ma continued, "See, that was not so hard. You had no reason to not answer the questions."

Van doors were slamming. Sabrina cranked and declared, "Let's go!" The protest resumed, "We can't leave Red." Sabrina stated the rock truth of her life, "He is in God's hands!" "But they might kill him!" "They might, but that won't remove him from God's hands."

"Let's go down to the parking lot. It is a much better place to talk!" They stood up. Red stared down at his flashlight all in pieces. He resisted leaving, for the flashlight light was needed for teleporting. "You won't ever use that flashlight again." Leaving the fragments on the table, they walked away from the restaurant toward the exit.

While in an obscure hall, Gene declares, "This is far enough." "Ma asked, "Why?" For the first time, she was not following Gene's train of thought. "Teleportation has always happened in the dark." "Oh, yeah!" joined in Gus, "They teleported in thunderstorms at night!" "It was night when we saw him magically hop." "We are definitely not going outside to the darkness." Now all three looked squarely at Red, "Now tell us how to teleport." Gus continued to be quiet in the probing of Red. Gene asked, "Ma, do we know anyone in Hughville?" Red gasped as the idea of someone kidnapping his daughter. "No!" A sigh of relief slipped out of Red. "No, but my brother. He knows someone. From the stories, that person is mean. He is such an inspiration in effective cruelty." "Now, now, now!" Boasted, Gene, "Contact your brother to have her picked up immediately. I remember some of those stories now! He will have so much fun."

Red gave in, "Okay, okay! I will tell you, but don't contact him." A big smile flirted with Gene's face, "See, I told you there was no point in resisting." "Part of the answer is in that conditioner bottle. Put a drop of conditioner on your finger." Gene commanded, "Ma, put a drop of that conditioner on your finger." "You're crazy if you think I am going to put a drop of that stuff on my finger." They both looked at Gus, "What do you think I am, dispensable? If one of us dies from a poison, it is okay if it is me? I thought you loved me more than that."

Red said nothing, but he knew they just might come up with his plan for him. In a serious voice, Gene unwrapped countless layers of suspicion. "Anyone, who can teleport can easily get poison. I know what you are trying to do. You want us to poison ourselves." Red interjected, "Let's go outside. I have something I want to show you." Ma stood firm, "Two things are not going to happen. We will not let you get in the dark where you can teleport, and we are most definitely not going to let you poison us." Frustration was invading Gene, "Call your uncle!" Red spoke again, "Put a drop of conditioner on your finger! Each of you!" Ma declared, "You think you can make us poison ourselves. How stupid do you think we are?"

Gus never joined in when ma and Gene terrorized people. Now he was extra sullen. It dawned on him for the first time that his family was willing to let him die.

Ma smiled, "I know how to get Red to talk." Gene asked so politely, "How is that my dear Ma?" Every poison has an antidote. We give him the poison, and we won't let him have the antidote until he reveals the secrets of teleportation." "Why Ma, that is a brilliant idea." Red interjected, "Why don't we just go outside? I have something I want to show you out there." "Not a chance!" "Let's go outside." Ma demanded, "Give me your finger!" Red resisted giving his finger and he started wrestling to get away. Gene commanded, "Ma, call your brother!" Red quit and declared, "Ok! Ok!" He put out his finger. With all his might, he fought the smile back.

Ma popped open the conditioner lid. She looked at the dark, gross color. "This ain't conditioner." She turned the bottle upside down and squeezed out a drop. As soon as the drop hit the skin, all the butterfly particles just vanished leaving a clear beige moisture. Ma commanded, "All right now rub it in!" Red evicted a huge sigh. He took his thumb and rubbed in the moisture until the cream disappeared. Red asked, "Please let me wash my finger?" "No!" "Please! Please!" "No!" "Tell us how to teleport." Red shoved out his finger and spoke, "Look what it is doing to my finger." They looked, but do not see anything out of the ordinary. "Can't you see?" "It won't be long now." "I don't see anything." "Do you?" "No!" "Give me my phone and I will show you." He snatched his phone, and flipped it on and pointed the light at his finger.

All of a sudden, the world stopped. The two men and the women were frozen in time. Red placed his finger under the light. In ma's rigid hand, was Red's billfold, he worked it out and shoved it in his pocket. Enclosed in her other hand was the bottle of conditioner. Red tried to bend her finger, but her flesh was as solid as granite. He realized that he could not open her hand. He ran away leaving the bottle in her grasp.

Upon arriving at his bedroom, he opened the door. He peeked into the butterfly cage, and the rest of the paper insects were dead. He set his light down. From downstairs he heard screaming. "He teleported out!" "He's gone!" Red with all urgency grabbed a glove and yanked it up the hand. He lunged forward, and opened his book. He set it down in front of himself. He snatched the cage, flipped open the hatch and shook out the butterflies onto his book. He closed the book gently. He retrieved a rubber band, stretched it, and locked the book closed.

He heard pounding on his door, come out, "Red! We know your teleporting skills are minimal. You can't run from us. Red yells back, "Coming!" He picks up his phone, and quickly scribbles a text. The whole time, he heard banging on the door. Come out, now!" "Okay!" He placed his finger back over the light. He opened the door, and a giant corpse blocked the exit. Red shoved, the statue tilted and fell over.

CHAPTER 17
ON THE RUN

Amy moaned, "I haven't had a good night sleep in forever." She reached for her phone to read the text that Red sent, then her arm dropped – sleep had won.

Red arrived at the airport by a taxi. He strolled up to his travelling companions. Unmasked and ungloved were the two super-diligent. "Oh, I see, you were able to ..." Red threw his hand in the "Shh!" position in front of his mouth. That did not keep the other cohort from talking, "Why that place jumping thing ..." Red violently wiggled his hand in front of his mouth. She took the hint and silenced.

Red roamed over and sat beside Sabrina. She whispered softly, "I am glad that you jumped out." "Thank you! Those bad guys also have the ability to be hoppers as well." "Oh! So, what does that mean?" "It means that they can teleport anywhere." The two ladies started again, "Don't you think we should tell the police?" "Yes, the police!" "Tell them what? ... The control for this power will devour us. Once they realize that teleportation is real, we will be thrown in some obscure place never to be seen again." "Oh, my!" "Oh, my, indeed!"

Amy was back asleep. The blaring of her phone cracked the heavy slumber. In a daze, she fumbled for her phone. In a slurred voice she answered, "Helloo!" "I'm hungry, I thought I would grab me some juice, and some potato chips. What are you doing up?" "Hunh? Is this Zach?" "Yes!" "Why are you calling me? It is the middle of the night." "Well, you don't have time for a snack?"

"Why?" "Did you read the text from Red?" "What text? Oh, that one! I fell back asleep." "You should read it." "Made enemies! Pack quickly and leave. What does that mean?" "You should leave very soon!" "What kind of enemies?" "Amy! Don't stop to think. He is fearing for your life. Get out!" As Amy quickly dressed, she quizzed "Where are you Zach?" "I am out of town with my mom at a baby shower." All of a sudden, glass broke. A split moment later, a faint crackling was heard as the glass clapped with the floor. "Too late!" With an alarmed voice, "Too late what?" "They are here!" "Get out!!"

Amy picked up her wallet. She darted swiftly to the door and peeked out. Standing right in front of her was a giant wall of a man. His back was turned as he was looking in the room across the hall. She ran to the window, she unlatched it, and yanked it upwards. All of a sudden, the rumbling fortress yelled, "I found her. She is trying to escape through a window."

Panic pulsated through her as she stared at the screen. The tiny little cross sections of screen appeared to her as giant crossbars of a prison. She lunged into them with all her strength not knowing if the mesh would impede her escape. Her head and knees thumped into the mosquito repellant sheet. She felt the pressure; and all of sudden, it popped out of her way. Great relief flooded her body as she felt like she was escaping, the immediate threat. All of a sudden, she felt a hand against her back. The hand slid off giving the feeling that her body would have been freed, then she felt her shirt squeezing her body. In a brief moment, she found herself dangling in mid-air. Her mind flashed to a kitten caught by the mane of the neck totally powerless to defend herself. "I got her!" squealed her captor. She wondered, how could a man so big and so strong, have such a wimpy voice?

Determination to live overcame her. She spun and glued her feet to the wall, and jumped – well, sort of. The hulk inside the house swayed ever so slightly by her strength as he was barely persuaded to lose his balance. As if in super-slow motion, he tipped forward and took a small step forward. His shoulders and head gently bumped into the window. Her legs straightened until the house arrested his movement, her legs stalled only slightly straightened. The giant laughed in his squeaky voice, "You thought you could get away. Come to me my darling." An eerie stomach bellow laugh crackled out of him.

Another voice intruded into the crisis from around the corner, "I'm comin,' I'm comin'!" The horror struck her, as soon as the voice would arrive, all hopes of escape would be doomed. Stuck in a motionless face down position, she looked back. His grip in one hand was far stronger than both of her legs. She was snared by the backside of her shirt forcing her to be face down. Without the ability to even face that tree trunk like arm, the chance of defending herself was zero. That other voice, the thundering one really scared her for it was deep and rich, "I'm Comin'! I'm comin'!" Using her feet against the wall, she twisted with all her might.

She swiped behind her with her arm to grab ahold of his forearm; but she missed, so she flailed at it again. On the second attempt, she grabbed her captor's arm and pulled with all her might to turn some more. In her other hand was her phone. She reared as far back as possible to strike with all her force. Her phone was protruding out of her hand like an ax. She identified his most vulnerable target. In one great snapping motion, she drove her phone's short end into the back of the man's hand. The casing struck bone and awakened the long tendons with a supercharged shock. "AHH!" squealed the overgrown muscle, but his grip hung firmly. She realized that she could not break the death grip for she was fighting too much power. Yet, without a pause, she reared back again to deliver more of the same. On her way down, the man in the window envisioned another burning blow to the vulnerable side of his hand.

He released his grip on her shirt, spun his hand, and reached upwards to grab her hand. She realized too late that she was trading one trap for another. Her arm was already in motion. Before she could react, she felt his grip around her wrist. What was not fully anticipated was her partially coiled legs were in launch mode. As soon as he began to release, she began to vault, but it was not enough. Her efforts to reverse her motion laid her wrist into his fingers. His thumb was barely able to reach, so he drove it deep into her soft tissue. Once again, she was locked in an immovable claw, his strength more than cemented his grip.

With the other hand, the ogre grabbed her heel closest to the window. She discovered that she did not have the power to break one firm grip, much less two. She pulled his hand to her face. She crunched his thumb with her teeth. The man hollered and shook his bit hand free.

Her foot, however, was still firmly held. She sprung forward. She landed with a thud in the middle of her back. Her foot was far bigger than her ankle giving the aggressor an easy hold. She stomped his hand with one foot while pulling with the other. A smile overtook his face because he knew she could not escape. The unexpected happened – his grip was technically around the shoed foot. The foot covering was held firmly, but the foot was free to leave. Liberated, she sprung up and ran with all her might.

She took one glance at the big voice to see a relatively little man. His words changed from, "I'm comin'!" to "I got her!" She darted through the bushes and changed directions hoping to slow him down. She took five full strides then darted back through the hedge only to sprint back in the direction she had come from. She was hoping to pick up her shoe as she ran by, but it was not there. She sprinted past her house and toward the back alley. She knew that she could hide in someone's yard and she would probably be safe. All she had to do was jump a fence before being seen. The third house down the alley had a lower cinderblock wall. She ran up to it, drove a foot waist high into the wall, and jumped upwards. She grabbed ahold with her fingertips.

With her feet, she tried to push up, but they kept slipping. She found herself hanging by the smallest of grips. She let go and continued to sprint away.

She felt trapped, the fences were too high for her to cross. She looked back and saw no one. With excitement, she thought, "I almost made it!" then a dog started barking. As she neared the end of the block, her head rotated to see if she was being pursued. Her heart sank, the nimble man was galloping at a speed far greater than her own. She knew she could never outrun him. She had to find safety. She reached the end of the alley. She left a residential neighborhood to enter into a business district. Everything was open without walls and with large parking lots.

If she could just disappear before he turned the corner, she felt she still had a chance. The next business was a gas station. She thought, "If I could just turn the corner and find a place to hide, I will be fine." As she attained the gas station, she looked back, he was not yet there. She was safe. Before she turned the corner, she heard the rumblings of a souped-up pick-up truck. She peeked around the corner. To her horror, there was the very same black truck that was in front of her house. She was trapped. She retraced a few steps and slithered into the gas station. The monster truck with the oversized wheels pulled ever so slowly in front of the store and stopped. She stared as her pursuer walked to the driver's door. She knew they were trying to create a game plan. Just then the front door opened, and entered her three greatest nightmares. "Oh great! I'm doomed!" she moaned.

Amy completely hid without peeking so that no one could spot her unless they walked right up to her. She just sat down on the floor. A loud voice echoed, "Look what I've found! Why if it is not the Zach chaser?" "Did you make any progress with him?" "If she had, she would not be sitting in the middle of the floor all alone!" The other two echoes, "All alone!" Amy implored, "Please stop, the two men outside are trying to kidnap me." The hostilities continued, "You're kiddin' right?" "Why would anyone want to kidnap you?" "Especially you!" Just then the front door opened, ushering in the two men. "Them?" "Yes!"

CHAPTER 18
SHOOT 'EM UP

The three gals glanced at each other. "You want to take a bet?" "You're on!" "I'm in!" All three pulled out wads of cash. Two girls slapped their cash into the third girl's hand. They had always amazed Amy with great impromptu creativity as they devised new and more malicious plots. Somehow, they always found a way to hurt more than she could ever have imagined.

With that first glance, Amy knew they had decided on their devious plot. They had never paused before; Amy was certain that this was their grandest piece of treachery yet. So, it began, as the three girls began their march straight toward the men. "Couldn't land Zach!" "Nope, not a chance!" "She settles for just any guy she can find now!" Amy was begging in soft tones, "No, no, no, no!"

As they reached the door, the one who was holding the money bounced outward and the other two began to argue. "He did not say that!" "Oh, yes he did!" "You just didn't hear the full conversation." "He clearly said, 'You're the cutest!' To me!" "No way any guy would think you are prettier than me." "You are so jealous of me!" Gradually, their volume increased, until there were yelling drawing the attention of the whole store. "He did not say you are lovelier than me!" "My charm is irresistible!" Amy whispered, "No guy in their right mind would think that except … Zach … and the rest of the guys in school!" Amy started creeping toward the door.

"What is so charming about you? Except, I'll admit, your nose is adorable, but not to the point of being more enticing than me." "Girl, you're just dreaming. Although, I admit some guys have said, 'I could get lost in your eyes!'" Their trek continued even past the men. "You think you are cuter than I?" "Yes, I most definitely do!" The two men kept looking at the two then glancing around the store. The two gals took a step toward each other. "You want to put it to the test!" "Put it!" They were screaming as loudly as they could. One of the two young ladies stared at the two rough men for the first time, "Who do you think is prettier between us?" Clearly by now the men were a little rattled for their actions had become jerky. They looked at the first heart stopper, then glanced all over the room. They inspected the second, then too quickly, their eyes bounced around the room.

Amy softly emitted, "No way! Behaving over the top vain, yet perhaps caring! Maybe they just want to raise my hopes to dash them even further. Miracles do happen! I have to believe it now!" The scoundrels quit looking at the two damsels. With all the commanding presence she could muster, "Look at me when I talk to you!" "How dare you ignore us like that!" "She is trying to destroy me, and you don't care!" "Look at us!" Amy took that as her cue, she crossed the open center area crouched over. The men turned to look at the women. Amy pushed on the door, and the buzzer rang. The men launched themselves toward the door. Amy thrusted herself outwards. Up against the curb was this fancy car with the passenger door open. Amy peered in knowing exactly who she would see while still on the run. Her third tormenter was staring her down motioning rapidly for her to come. Amy jumped in and closed the door as she landed. The driver flipped open her hand and revealed a wad of cash. "Here, this is all the money we have!" Amy just stared in disbelief. "Take it! Who do you think we are? Cruel women? ... Wait, don't answer that! You probably do."

The car raced down a couple of blocks, turned, continued racing forward a little bit then shuddered to a stop! The tone that Amy was familiar with had returned, "Get out! Now!" Amy was still in shock and unable to process the words that were even harsher than before, "Get out!" With much eagerness, she said, "Take these, you'll need them!" The one behind the wheel twisted, and raised her knees to the side while keeping her ankles together on the other. She slid her fingers behind her heels and popped off her shoes. The efficient sudden process stopped with two tennies in front of Amy's face. The parting words were so aptly spoken, "Take the shoes and money and go home. Get your car and ride ... and find Zach, he will take care of you!" Amy was still motionless.

"Go! Go now!"

Amy grabbed the shoes and hopped out. She spotted a parked car a few steps away. She darted in front of it and ducked. That little car she hated to see had been her refuge. She heard the crackling of the souped-up truck roaring up from behind. Terrified she muttered to herself. "Please don't stop! Please don't stop." She did not know if they had seen her get out or not. She quickly slapped on one shoe, and waited. Amy looked around to find an escape if they should stop. She saw nothing! Her mind was empty. There was no back-up plan. The truck blared its ridiculous thunder and chased that vulnerable gal. As soon as the truck passed, Amy rolled around the car. She sat at the other end and replaced the second shoe. As the sound of the truck faded, she stated, "If they catch her, they will kill her!" In disbelief she continued, "My worst enemies gave me their money, shoes off one of them and are risking their lives for me! ... And, I didn't even say thank-you." Amy got up and walked away with a new pair of shoes to her on the feet, a phone in one hand, a shoe in the other, and two fingers curled around a wad of cash.

Back in the store, the men darted out. They had parked far enough from the entrance so that the cameras would not pick up their truck. They raced out with one hand on their hoodies so that their head covering would not fly off. Even in the open, they were experts at being invisible.

The two gals were motionless except they were finger sprinting. Each with a phone in hand, they were quickly unfolding the next part of their plan. When finished they looked at each other. "The bet is on!" "Rock it!"

Nine minutes after the chase began, the truck was on the heels of the muscle car. The little guy on the passenger side, rolled down his window and shot. The lead driver screamed, "Don't hit me! Don't hit me! Don't hit me!" She dropped as low as she could while still barely being able to see over the dashboard. Another thunderous ripping of metal filled the air. "Do it again! Don't hit me! Don't hit me! "Do it again!" The car screamed in pain again, and the soprano voice squealed out one more time, "Do it again! Don't hit me! Don't hit me! "Do it again!" Once more, a thundering clash hits the car as she weaved a little to mess up the aim upon her.

Once again, the phone was stared at? "Why do you keep staring at your device, Red?" "I am just trying to find WIFI so that I can text my daughter again. The airport just does not seem to have free service." Sabrina asked, "What are you wanting to tell her?" "Tell her? Tell her?" Sabrina was surprised by the intensity of his response. "My attackers have sent someone to our house to kidnap her. I want to know if she is safe." "Oh, my! How awful!" Mickey conjectured, "You can't go home! You can't go back to work! You are fugitives – both of you!" "I know!" Sabrina inquired, "So, what are you going to do?" "I don't know. My life is over like I know it for they will never stop hunting us down!"

The ruckus could be clearly heard for the popping of the gun with the piercing of the car competed with the rumbling of the engine. It is late at night, late enough that everyone should be at home in bed.

"Made it!" squawked the dainty voice. She rushed into a parking lot. The truck was hot on her tail, and slid in right behind her. All of a sudden, the parking lot came to life. Hundreds of headlights popped on. Every horn blared. A line of pick-up trucks formed an arc, facing the entrance. Young men in the beds of the pick-up trucks jumped. In their hands were shot guns, rifles, even quite a few had BB guns. Several had bows. One even had a fantasy light saber. Anything to look intimidating. The showdown arena was so loud that the rumbling of the black truck could no longer be heard. The little car raced through the one gap opening. Immediately, the gap was covered as a big farm tractor filled in. The once-so-bold assailants squealed to a stop. They couldn't talk as the cars blared their horns and engines. The headlights were so blinding making the line of shooters seemingly ghostly. For a little bit nothing happened, then the wheels started to smoke, as the two human hunters retracted. As soon as they started fleeing, the place erupted in cheers. Horns celebrated in quick short bursts.

Had there been any questions before, the three young ladies had become the darlings of the school. They ran in front of everyone, and motioned for people to come. The photographer raced out. Quickly everyone posed. The three yelled, "Tough pose!" The weapons pop out, the guys puffed out their chests, and flexed their arms. "Silly pose!" Everyone spun around and stuck out their booty. "Trophy pose!" The tractor started spitting, slowly at first, then at normal cadence as it cranked. It pulled in front of the trucks sideways.

The car poked through the newly created gap, drove a lit bit away, then returned to show off the bullet holes. The back window was frosted over and partially gone. The students jumped on the tractor racing for the best spots. Students seize every available nook until the tractor was completely covered. Others stood being pressed inwards until the pressing surrendered no more space. Many of the smaller students squatted and sat in front. No space was left except directly facing the rear of car. The three-gals direct traffic with great urgency until all had found a place. The trio hopped on the back of the car laying belly up on the trunk. To achieve their niche, they contorted backwards so that their knees rested on the top of the car, and their elbows were at the back edge of the trunk. They let their feet dangle each differently. They did their thing once again. All three had their bodies perfectly parallel, yet each was in a completely different yet fully alluring pose – unity, yet unique grace. Time was short as they heard the sirens blare, much has been accomplished, but there was more business to attend to.

Two girls rolled on their backs and the third jumped across them. "Who do you think won the bet?" "I say we all did!" "Big winners!" The two below asked the shoeless on top? "Where's the money?" "That cheap gal took it. She even took my shoes!" "That is just like her!" "Wait till I get my hands on her!" They giggled and scrunched up.

They hopped off and greeted those who made the moment happen. A bunch of girls jumped around them, and a few guys. The group hug grew. They fluttered in the wind and shook back and forth. Quickly before the party was spoiled by the blue, they hugged one after another. Some of the more bashful guys sought no hugs, although they would dream about it for months if they did. Out came the fist bumps and high fives. The three limelight seekers, who planned their popularity, also were generous in sharing stardom. Finally, came guys who were so terrified of being in their presence; not just with them, but with any female. At that moment, the girls were at their finest, "What you did was really brave today!" "You chose to face armed bandits!" "You are a hero!" Finally, one guy came up too bashful to even look up. A crooked index finger found its way under his chin and lifted up his head. Words, he would remember the rest of his life were spoken, "You helped save my life today, thank you!" On one side of the face, a smile cracked, the head dropped and the fella walked away. For this chap, that was the grandest expression of emotion in public in a very long time.

CHAPTER 19
FUGITIVES

During the one-stop layover still far from home, a tear slipped out of Red's eye. He hopped up and walked away so that the others would not see him cry. As he wandered alone, a familiar voice rang out above the ruckus of the airport, "Hotdogs! Hotdogs! Anyone want hotdogs?" Red rushed following the invisible voice trail. Sure enough, in front of him, was a hotdog stand. "Would you like a hotdog? You have not had a good meal in a long time." "How did you get here?" "What do you mean? I have had my stand here for the last thirty years? Where do you think I came from?"

Red realized that the argument was pointless. He stared at the lightning and butterflies painted all over the cart. Red declared, "You are right! My adventure has begun and it is costing me everything!" "What do you mean everything?" "I can't go back home. I can't return to my job or any job because I am being hunted. My daughter is also a fugitive, she can't go to a university, marry, or carry on a normal life unless …" "Unless what?" "Unless she is already captured." "Your adventure has begun. And it is costing you everything. Are you ready to pay?" "How can God make me lose everything like that?" The vendor handed Red his hotdog. "Be of good courage and He shall strengthen your heart, o you who hope in the Lord, Psalms 31:24." "BLAM" popped a loud noise on the other side of the concourse. Stunned, Red swiveled his head. He did not see anything so he immediately oscillated back to face Monkabe.

Not so much to his surprise, the cart and the peculiar man were gone. "Teleported!"

Amy entered an all-night department store. She shopped for new clothing so that she would not be so easily spotted. She muttered, "I've spent my whole life trying to look pretty and catch the eye, now I am trying to look invisible. She gazed down at her phone as she received a new text. "No, no, no, no, no, no, no, no, no, no! Any other plan, but that, Dad!" Frantically, she texted back, "Yes, Dad, I am fine! Some men chased me for a little bit. What have you done to make people so angry?" "Nothing, nothing – nothing doesn't make people try to kidnap you." "What do you mean you can't tell me the story." "When will all this end?" "What do you mean, 'Right now, it has no end.'" "So, what are we going to do?" She slid the phone into her pocket and mumbled the last text received, "This isn't ours to solve; ours is to trust." She paused for the longest while before finishing the quote. "No matter how things go – reach to heaven and taste the sweetness of victory." She finished with a few words of her own. "Dad, you're the best! Mine is to trust. I will be content not seeing good for the goodness of heaven will find me!"

Sitting in an all-night restaurant was a hooded figure. Poking out of the hood was a ball cap. The clothes were dark colored and loose-fitting. If the person were to stand up, the jeans would sag. The sleeves would have overgrown the hands leaving an indistinguishable figure that could not be seen. The longing to be invisible had claimed another. The diner's door opened, and the figure ducked the head out of fear. A man entered with some sort of work uniform. He wandered to the front and ordered. With his back turned, she ratcheted up her head just enough to retrieve a glimpse of the newcomer.

Ten minutes later, the door angled again wide enough for one to enter comfortably, but two squeeze in. A young man had his arm curled around his fascination keeping her locked to him. He ordered an ice-cream and picked up two wrapper coated spoons.

It would not be noticed if one hundred scary people had entered the room, for the two love birds had eyes only for each other.

Another hour or so passed, and others came, and the loner had barely moved at all. The observed had lost some of its fascination. Finally, Amy had time to unwind. The restful solitude was anything but calming. The past few hours swarmed like a tempest. She remembered Zach waking her up with his phone call for her to flee. Before she even had time to take-off, in came a giant of man who caught her. An accomplice was zooming to grab her as well. She fled for her life. She had to buy new clothes to be invisible. No place, no location was safe. She had become a fugitive.

What about her dad, Red? He was in a foreign country somewhere running for his life – that is if he was not caught or dead. The life she cherished was destroyed. The time to think was not prized for the time alone magnified the troubles. The time alone turned two switches – the need to be independent without a man was turned off, and the desire to walk these difficult times with a man, a certain man was turned on.

The door opened still again, and the hooded loner quickly retreated into her shell. Both arms dashed back into the sleeves, and the head ducked. She chose to not be seen so as anyone who entered could not recognize her. She was only willing to peek when she was certain that she was safe. A young man entered, he turned and headed straight her way. He stopped, and bent over far enough to look under the hood. To do so, his head skimmed the tabletop. "Oh, it's you." He spoke while smiling.

Zach still was not sure where the relationship stood between him and Amy even if there was one more than the necessity of a crisis. Upon the first glimpse of her face, Zach saw a woman shell-shocked by the day's troubles. Zach thought about playing it safe; then he realized, he longed to do things right in a way he would never regret. The hood was down past her nose. He reached his hand under the head covering. His pinkie side of hand landed upon her hair line. With one slow and efficient stroke, his hand flowed all the way back to the crown of the head. He was not done for he continued down to her neck dragging that ugly hoody off her head. He had uncovered her head to give her back some dignity even if only for a moment. Then he realized he was not done, there was something he had to say, "Red was right, you are beautiful!" She arose quickly. She emerged from her station with arms up, the hands slid past his head then wrapped around. She gave him not just a courteous hug, but a bear hug. Zach in his boyish charm spoke, "When you are in this close, I can't see your beauty." Involuntarily, she giggled.

Amy confessed, "You are every bit as skilled as your three friends." After some silence, Zach continued, "You seriously compare my skills to the three magnificent ones?! That is such an incredible compliment!" Amy asked, "Are they safe? Did they get away from those two terrifying guys?"

He picked his own pocket and displayed a phone, "Look at the posts from the three wonders! Look at this one! Each girl is kissing a different bullet hole." As always, they displayed much flair. One was below, kissing the air right in front of the hole. Another was leaning forward at a forty-five stopping just shy of the crater. The last one was on the hood with puckered lips. "They even have audio. Listen!" He hit the sideways triangle, and out came a conversation that Amy had heard in person. "He did not say that!" "Oh, yes, he did!" "You just didn't hear the full conversation." "He clearly said, 'You're the cutest! To me!" "No way any guy would think you are prettier than me." "You are so jealous of me!" Zach pitched in, "They recorded their whole charade."

They have had twelve million hits so far. They are famous worldwide. They even included these pictures. The shoeless driver was standing almost directly facing the camera. A man with his back turned had a finger in her face. "The caption says, 'Grounded … forever!!!'"

Zach pointed to another. A woman was sobbing into her hands while giving her daughter the cold shoulder. Zach read,

> "It said, 'I should have thought. I could have been killed.' Her mother was really mad. Here is another, she is tiny compared to the giant policemen all around her. A woman cop in the middle was talking to her. 'You could have gotten everyone killed!' They are so classy! They are not even defending themselves; rather, they are expressing the views of those who are angry at them."

CHAPTER 20
KIDNAPPED!

R ed left the restricted area of the airport. He walked briskly hoping to get out safely. He arrived at the baggage claim signs and walked right by them. He continued his march until he reached the airline counters. There waiting for him was Zach, and he rushed across the grand room to lead Red to safety. Before he could attain Red's side, a mountain of a man and a little wiry one slid on either side of Red. They guided him quickly outside, and they disappeared. Zach was standing there trying to figure out which way to go. Somebody tapped him on the shoulder, and stated, "Red wanted you to have this." Zach jumped and stared at the boy; Mickey offered him a book held together by a rubber band. As soon as Zach received the book, the boy took off.

A woman with long blond hair and sunglasses moved close to Zach, "I thought you were getting Red." "Two men took him. A big, tall one and a wiry short one." "Oh, I know them!" "At least, they were caught on camera." "Maybe, they were in obvious disguises." Zach turned and stared at Amy, "You look cute in your disguise." Zach then grew serious, "Sorry about your dad."

Sometime later, a van pulled up to a remote house by a lake. The driver opened his door, hopped out and did the chauffeur thing – he opened the back door. As the finest of drivers would do, he aided the occupant to unfold from the vehicle; except without all the etiquette, he grabbed the figure by the armpit and yanked. Red slammed into the door since he was sprung by a great force. "You owe an apology growled the driver. You pay now!"

Red was dragged into the house. Red resisted a little – just enough to size up his captor, and little enough to hope to avoid a beating. The little rebellion was just to test the strength of the ogre. Red thought he rebelled, but his pulling back was so weak in comparison that it appeared as if he had done nothing at all. Red understood that he was powerless to fight the man.

A detective interred the room. Amy and Zach stood in great anticipation. "I am detective Œil. That is spelled, o with an e attached, i, l. It is French for the word eye. I am detective eye. I was assigned to your case, yesterday, when those men shot up your town. The three young ladies could have died trying to save you. In fact, those acts ended up putting all the young people at risk for they all came to your rescue. I have worked the most challenging cases all over the country, and I have never seen anything like this one. Would you mind telling me what is going on, young lady?" Amy was flabbergasted by the introduction. Immediately, she did not care much for this detective. She knew he was trying to exert control, but she was the victim and not the criminal. "I really don't know what is going on. I was hoping you would tell me." "If you withhold evidence, it is a crime. Embedding! Conspiracy! Those charges can come into play."

All of a sudden, Zach remembered that he has a book in his possession – the very book that a lad thrust at him and disappeared. Zach griped the book harder. He twisted it in his hand, then he tucked it under his leg without saying a word.

Amy attempted to calm the situation. "Please tell me what is going on? Why did they take my father? Why was he afraid? Please explain things!" The detective stared at her. He said nothing, cocked his head in a different direction, and remained quiet. He picked up the remote and turned to the screen. He showed the video of the abduction. Two men swarmed Red; they escorted him out to the parking lot. They shoved Red into a car, and left.

Amy interjected at the end, "So you can identify the two and the car, can't you?" "Unfortunately, the car was stolen and the men's disguises make identification impossible so far. We are doing all we can. What we need to know is what Red was involved in?" Amy answered, "He went on a spiritual pilgrimage." "You know there are no major spiritual sites anywhere near his destination." Once again, Amy felt like a criminal. "We will keep his bags to look for clues."

The officer turned toward Zach and asked, "What is your involvement in all of this?" "I am with her. I am just keeping her company." "Girlfriend? Fiancé? Partner?" Amy spoke in Zach's place, "We just met, but I would be honored if he would call me his girl-friend." Zach spoke the detective, "Girl-friend … most definitely girl-friend." The detective evaluated the situation. "Red had been taken hostage! And you, my son, maybe in severe trouble if you continue to hang out with her."

Ma squealed out, "You thought you could run away from us! Well, surprise. You are caught now, and there is no escape." Red retorted, "Even if I did escape, there is no place to go. You have sabotaged my life." Gene ramrodded Gus with his elbow, "See, Red is starting to understand!" Gene was so full of glee that he was possessed by the greatest smile. Gus grabbed his ribs and sputtered, "Herh, herh, herh, herh!"

Red bluntly asked, "What is your plan with teleporting?" Gene blurted, "Tell him, Ma!" "We plan on robbing banks. We teleport in, and teleport out with the loot and no one will be able to figure this out! We will become the greatest bandits of all time." Gene concluded, "We will pull stunts that no other robber has ever done. We will be legends." The wiry little man who had chased Amy on foot, snapped to attention. His oversized companion asked, "What is it, scarecrow?" "Doughboy, I just realized, we know today's armored car route. Stealing from it should be the simplest kind of teleporting." Doughboy interjected, "I won't believe this teleporting stuff until I see it!"

CHAPTER 21
MASTERING TELEPORTATION

On their way out, Amy asked, "So what do you think we are?" "You know I am I guy and we guys don't like to talk about our feelings." "Oh" came the deflated response. Zach continued, "If I told you the truth that I think about you all the time and you have sabotaged my sleep, then I would make myself so vulnerable. So, to be safe, I won't tell you that I have been wishing you were mine." Amy responded, "You are so adorably charming."

The gang was sitting in a van arguing. Ma, "How does teleport work anyway?" Gene became defensive, "How would I know? I have never done it before." Ma growled out a question, "Red, how does teleporting work anyway?" Red stated, "Give me a drop of that conditioner and I will demonstrate." Ma retorted, "We know better this time. Under no circumstances are you going to get a drop." Gene turned to Gus, "All you have been is a bag of hot air, you have not helped us solve anything." Gus cordially responded, "Then let me be helpful. Red is there a weight limit to teleporting? If there is Gene here will never, ever – I mean never, ever, ever be able to teleport." Gene retorted, "You are not helping at all! All you are doing is stirring the pot." "Looking at you, you have had plenty of practice stirring the pot!"

Just then, the armored car pulled up. Ma declared, "Shut up the both of you! Here is our chance – we need to figure out this teleporting stuff right now. Red, I am warning you, you had better tell us." Red said nothing. Gene spun around in the van surprising well for a man his size. His face could be clearly seen, and it said plenty – he was sunburnt red. For a long time, hated and jealousy had been burning at his soul. Now, with a chance to radically change his life, the festering decay consumed Gene. "You had better do as you are told, right now! I mean, right now!!!" Red just sat there. He had crushed so many butterfly wings energizing that sample bottle of conditioner with so much power. All Red hoped for was the wasting of a significant amount before they really figured out how to stop time.

Red just stared at Gene. "Tell me now!" Red was harnessed in his spot by the seatbelt. "Now!" Nothing but silence. All of a sudden Gene punched Red. The prisoner never saw it coming. Even if he did, there was nothing much he could have done. Red's head flew backward. Without trying to protect himself, Red just slumped over to one side. Without pausing, Gene cocked back and struck again. This time with Red being slumped over, and not much of the face could be seen, the blow did not strike squarely. Infuriated, Gene snapped and struck again into the soft portions of the chest. Ma leaned in between the two men, "Stop! Stop! Stop!" Gene began another strike but held himself in check to avoid hitting his mother. "You knocked him out with your first blow. Beating him more won't help!"

Within Gus, a yearning had been growing. For the first time in his life, he had been around someone who suffered much and yet was at peace. While unconscious, Red somehow ignited hope in Gus. His admiration for Red emerged in pure sarcasm, "Red is not red. He is already turning black and blue." He looked up at Gene, "Oh, look, Gene! You are most definitely Red." To rub things in, he repeated himself, "Red is black and blue; and Gene is a pure Red. Imagine that!" Gene lunged at Gus with all his might. His fist ignited at full power. Gus flinched and the fist flew harmlessly by. Ma jumped on Gene's back to stop him.

Ma grabbed the conditioner container. She placed a drop on her index finger. She ordered, "Give me your finger!" They both complied and received their droplets. "How hard can figuring this out be? Red figured it out quickly; we can do the same. Get out your phones, so that we can activate this potion. They both followed her orders.

Ma turned on her light. All of a sudden, everything outside stopped. One man was walking with one foot off the ground. Well, he was not really walking anymore for he was nothing more than a frozen statuette. "Oh, so that's it. This goop makes time stop and it appears to be teleporting." She was still too angry with her sons to look back. "C'mon! Follow me!" She fumbled with the door since her hands were occupied between the light and the drop, yet she managed to bumble her way out. Ma boldly walked up to the money carrier, and stared him in the face. His expression with someone in his face changed no more than any good statue would. "Gene, do you see this? He is totally frozen." Gene did not answer. "Gene! Gene?" All of a sudden Ma realized something had gone wrong. "Gus?" She scooted back to the van in a fury. She had left the door open for the others to follow so she hopped back in without having to figure out how to overcome that obstacle. She yelled, "Why did you not follow me?" She glared at them with anger then realized that her sons were as frozen as everyone else.

She extinguished her light. As soon as off happened, her sons snapped out of it. The third man in the metal carriage remained unconscious. Ma accused, "Why did you not turn on your lights with me and go outside?" Gene responded, "We are still waiting on you to give orders to turn on our lights and go outside." Ma explained, "I figured out teleporting. It is so amazing. It is not really teleporting at all. Time stops. Everything freezes. I got out of the car, and went over to the money carrier, and stared him eyeball to eyeball. He didn't even blink or move at all. I called to you to see it, but you did not come." "Really? You went all the way out there with time frozen!? Oh, we can do this! Taking what should belong to us is going to be so easy. Are you ready to go back out?" They looked up, and the van was already pulling away. Gene declared, "We will get them at the next stop."

Zach and Amy were walking around the park. Amy started a conversation, "Where should we go?" "I don't know!" "I mean, we have to do something to find Pa." "Yeah, but what?" "Where are we going to spend the night? "I don't know!" "Are we going to spend the night in the car?" "I don't know!" "Do you have any plans?" "I'm thinking!" Zach stated, "We do not have good answers, but one thing will make this better. Can I have your hand?" There they stood a foot apart staring each other down hand in hand. In the distance between them was a hotdog stand.

On the way Ma reasoned, "Whoever turns their light on first freezes the others, so whoever is awake must put light on the others." Gene added, "That is what I was thinking!" "So, should the alert one share the light or turn the other person's light on?" "It is not that complicated, let's just do it!"

They came to a stop. Before Ma had a chance to follow her train of thought, Gene changed the subject to avoid the pointlessness. "It is time, are you ready?" spat out Ma. "We will get them this time!" They each held out a finger. Ma released a drop on each tip. Red looked up, he had to turn his face because the left was so swollen that the eyelid would not open. A weak smile caught a corner of his mouth. He dropped his head back down so that no one would know he was awake.

They turned on their phone lights, and the world stopped once again. Gus declared, "You weren't lying, Ma. Everything does stop. This is so amazing." Gene exclaimed, "Well, I will be a monkey's uncle. The legends of teleportation are real. The legend will be even more amazing when we get some of that money that we deserve. Let's go!" They hopped out and rushed over to the money. There was plenty of bags to pick-up, but they just fidgeted trying to figure out how to pick-up the money with occupied hands; one hand has a light on the other. Gene ordered, "Let's go back and do this right. We don't want to leave any money." They returned empty handed, closed the door, and started yelling at each other. Ma gritted, "See, we should have talked this out more!" Gene fired back, "How would talking more have helped? We could have talked forever and not anticipated having full hands. Besides, when you talk, all I ever hear is whining and complaining." By this time, they were all sitting in the van. Gene spoke again, "Ready, let's turn off our lights! See, I am talking! Happy?" He turned off his light, and the other two kept their lights on. Gene was frozen and the other two looked at him, then at each other. Gus concluded, "I like him better this way." Ma concurred, "Me, too!"

Zach and Amy walked past the hotdog stand. They were dejected. Monkabe, "Have a hotdog to cheer your spirits!" "It will take a lot more than a hotdog to cheer us up." "Come here and let me tell you a secret." They just stood. "C'mon! Come closer." They each took a step forward. "Come much closer." Monkabe waved them in. They kept inching forward until they arrived at a secret distance, then Monkabe spoke. "When lightning strikes, time stands still." "What does that mean?" "You won't know until you are in the middle of the storm." Amy declares, "We are in the middle of a storm!" "Ahhh, the storm is only starting!" Amy, "How is that cheering our spirits?" "Troubles are coming to claim you!" "You do a lousy job of cheering up!" "For now, yes it seems! Without a storm, there would be no need for a miracle." "What are you trying to say?" "You make no sense!" "The storm will interpret my words. The storm is becoming much thicker. Things will grow much darker, but keep looking for the miracle for a heavenly wondrous act is your way out."

Ma declared, "I think we should put the dot on our foreheads so that we can use one hand." Gene searched for any reason to correct his mother, "So you mean we have to hold our phones all the way up to our forehead the entire time." Gus chipped in, "With our hands in front of our faces blocking our view!"

Gene responded again, "That would be so annoying. How about putting the dot under our chin so that we do not have to raise our light hand so high." Ma retorted, "When we talk things out, you always have to have your way, but at least you are talking this time – that is an improvement." Ma pulled the bottle out of her pocket. Are you ready to place a drop under your chin?" Everyone stuck out a finger. She donated a dab to everyone. They immediately retrieved their fingers and rubbed under their chin until the ointment disappeared. Gene instructed, "Wait, just a moment more. Wait! Wait! Okay, you can turn on your lights." The previous times, whoever had turned on the light first had to help the other two. This time nothing happened when one turned on the lights one by one. Ma exclaimed, "It didn't work? How could it not work? It has got to work!" Gene said, "Try your finger where you put the stuff." Ma turned on her light right directly on her finger. Everyone stopped and became rigid. She stood up and worked her way until she was directly in front of Gene. Once she was a sheet of paper distance away from Gene, she turned off her light. Gene threw his phone and jumped back, "That is the most terrifying thing I have ever seen in my life." "You are just jealous that I teleported into someone's face first."

Mickey asked beyond hope, "Have they found Red, yet?" "No!" "So, he could still be alive." "You're right, he could very well be." "What about his daughter? Is she safe?" "I don't know, son." "I am sure she is hiding somewhere." "We need to help them!" "Red did not wish for us to." "He does not desire for them to come for us!"

Zach declared, "That hotdog hit the spot!" "Yeah, it did!" He questioned, "Did you pay for the hotdogs?" "No, did you?" "No!" "It was like he was just giving them to us!" "Maybe, he was!" "It seemed that way, but no vendor just gives away the food." "Do you want to go back and see him?" "Sure, let's go!" When they arrived, the cart was already gone.

Gene whined, "At this rate, we are going to run out of drops before we figure out the secrets of teleportation." Ma retorted, "Quit your whining and give me your chin." He tried to give her his double chin, but no matter how he turned his head, he could not position his chin upside down. He conceded, "Just put it on the front of my chin instead of under my chin." With fire in her voice, she rumbled, "Oh no, you wanted the drop under your chin, genius, so you will give me the underneath of your chin!" "I can't!" "Oh, yes you can! Do what it takes!" Gene looked at her and realized it was hopeless. He stood up, and looked all around. He was very obviously confused. Gus snorted, "You have had no problem raising your nose and chin way up in the air before, what is the matter now?" "Shut-up!" Now Gus was a little startled for Gene always has a more clever, meaner answer than shut up. "If I don't shut up, are you going to try to knock me out again?" "Just shut-up!"

Gene made up his mind – he lowered the armrests on a middle row bucket seat. While standing leaning over, he faced backwards. He mounted the seat and armrests while holding on to the headrest. He was too stiff and too big for his rump to slide down between the handles, after he stalled, he let go of the head prop with one hand and let his body fall back as far as it could. With his free hand, he held on to the seat in front of him. He released his original handhold and grabbed the front seat with both hands. Gradually, he worked his hands down until they reached the floor. "Okay, I'm ready." Ma responded, "That took way too long, the armored bank is leaving. I just wanted to see you do it." "You would risk earning our life's fortune to watch me pretzel myself?" "It was worth every penny! C'mon, they are going to get away!"

Gene tried to get up, but he couldn't. He reached upwards to push the brace to the upright position. Gene's head was all red from the excessive blood. With his head on the floor, he had kept his neck rigid to avoid sliding downwards anymore. Already, he was starting to shake from exhaustion. With one side free from the armrest, he just allowed himself to fall over. His body slammed down hard shaking the whole van. Gus commented, "That was graceful!" "I told you to shut up and I mean it!" "Touchy!"

Zach wondered out loud, "Do you really think, the hotdog man knew what he was talking about?" "I don't know! It is the strangest thing. It was like I was believing everything he said, but not wishing to consider it the truth." "It was crazy! It was like he knew everything that was going on!" "I can't possibly think things can get a lot worse. Dad was taken hostage, and who knows if he is still alive. I can't go home for I am now a fugitive from criminals. I have lost everything and I have to live in hiding. How can things get a lot worse?" Zach wisely kept his mouth shut.

Ma exclaimed, "That was too easy. All we had to do was walk up to them, pick up everything, and leave. They had no clue. Let's go visit some banks. They are begging for our attention." "Right on, Sis; but first, let's go by the hardware store."

CHAPTER 22
THE ROBBERIES

Mickey begged his mom, "We have got to do something!" "What could we do?" "We have to do something!" "Why?" "They need our help!" "They need lots of help, but why us?" "You don't get it, Mom. Just forget it!" Mickey was very flustered. He was pacing, bouncing around the room. "Come here, Son!" He came slowly with head down. She continued, "You really want to help, don't you?" "Yes!" His mom hugged him tight just for a second, then she let him go! Mickey listened, "This is not about helping them, it is about trust." Sadness overcame, Mickey. As much as he did not desire to admit it, he knew that his mother had an answer he so needed to calm down. Sabrina continued, "If God is calling you to help, He would give you a way to make a difference, but He hasn't. Our Maker is waiting to love on you when you are ready. Are you tired of feeling helpless?" He just nodded.

Amy and Zach found their way to a coffee shop, and they were sitting there passing the time away. Amy asked Zach, "Why are you spending the day with me? They don't know you exist. You are free to leave and carry on your life." Zach turned and took hold of both hands, "You are my treasure! If I walk away from you now, I will be exceedingly poor. You are my life."

Mickey yelled, "Mom, Mom! Come here quickly. You have got to see this!" Sabrina half ran half walked to the den. "Look! Red's bad guys learned how to teleport." The bank president was being interviewed on TV. "I have never seen anything like this before. One moment, all the registers were full of cash, the next moment, they were empty. They drilled holes in all the safe deposit boxes, and emptied them. All in the twinkling of an eye. One moment everything was here and normal, the next everything was gone. I can't explain it!" Mickey exclaimed, "See, they made Red tell them how to teleport! They don't need Red anymore. They are going to kill him!" "Can they teleport without him?" "I don't know, Mom!" "Red never told me how to teleport!"

The bank president was about to continue, but the reporter interrupted. "I am sorry, but there is a late breaking development we must attend to." She turned around and faced the camera. "It is just in; another bank has been robbed in the same manner just moments ago."

Zach had been looking at the muted news with captions flowing. A word that zoomed by was "teleporting." "Wait, wait, wait! Teleporting!" He spoke even louder to the lady behind the counter. "Turn up the volume!" The announcer proclaimed, "A third bank has been hit within the last hour taking everything of value from the cash in the registers to the treasures in the safe deposit boxes." Amy moaned, "That is going to take precedent over our case. Nobody will be looking for dad, now!" "Are you kidding? They are the same ones who took Red." From the TV, "And now the police chief!" "Thank you. We know very little about these bandits. These robberies are different than anything ever seen before. The 'teleporters,' as we call them …" Zach yelled, "See, I told you they are the same ones." She looked at him puzzled. "What I did not tell you is that in the airport a boy ran up to me and handed me Red's book. He said, 'Here is the secret to teleporting!' Then, he ran off!" "Who was he?" "I don't know!" "Why did you not tell me this before?" "Too much was going o …" He stopped before tagging on the n. Zach couldn't resist turning a serious time into a pun. "I was just thinking about you!" She leaned over and kissed Zach gently on the cheek.

Red's face had grown uglier from the many beatings. "Why did you go to Africa, old man?" "I ..." Gene continued, "Wait, don't tell me that they had something you wanted. They met in unmarked buildings. Buildings with no name. Didn't you find it strange, Ma, that they would meet in tiny little buildings without a sign?" "I did! It took me a while to figure it out. They were not hiding who they are, but still they were nameless." "Would you like to tell us, Red, why they met in buildings without a name?" Red opened his mouth to speak, but Ma cut him off. She squeezed in close to where their noses almost touched. "Those weren't church buildings!" Gene cuts her off, "That is right, Ma! Church buildings have names. You are getting somewhere, what were they?"

Red opened his mouth again, and Ma overlayed her index finger vertically over his lips. "Shh! They were too poor to have church buildings. Those tiny little huts they met in, were homes, and not just any home." Gene interjects, "What do you mean, Ma? Those tiny little shelters were so inadequate. The heat from all those bodies – bodies that were forced to be so close that they touched." Ma jumped back in, "Two bodies so close one to another in the tropics feels suffocating, but a room full of bodies touching for lack of space with no AC, no fan, no window to let the heat blow out is ... is ..." "Is what Ma?" "Is so overwhelming that it makes people dizzy – an hour or more of singing, dancing to the music, makes people sway so much that they could easily ... easily ..." With a very agitated voice, "Could easily what, Ma? You have got to tell me?" "They could easily stumble and faint." "You mean they could just fall over from heat exhaustion?" "Absolutely! That kind of heat is so dangerous, they could die from that." "Without warning!" "Sure, they could look like they were fine, but then just drop over and be gone." Red knew they were right. Church with that kind of heat is most oppressive. Red knew what they were saying was true, he was just not sure what case they were building against him. All he really knew was he was in trouble.

CHAPTER 23
THE BUTTERFLY WING

Zach and Amy were waiting in the police station. Zach asked, "Should we open the book and see what was so important that people were willing to kill us over." "It must be some set of codes to access the teleporter. Look for handwritten numbers and gibberish."

Zach smiled and swung the book open, and the draft flowing into the vacuum caught a butterfly wing that took flight and escaped the book. The wing elegantly floated to the ground." Zach reached down to pick it up; and the wing, as soon as it touched his fingers, just disappeared." Startled Amy demanded, "Where did it go?" "I don't know, as soon as I touched it, it just disintegrated – there's nothing to pick up." Amy tried to console Zach, "Oh, it is alright! Just be careful and not let any more fall out." Zach turned the pages slowly and found no handwritten markings. "There is nothing! I don't get it!"

Just then, an officer walked up to them, "Please come this way!" Zach and Amy entered into the office of an officer who motioned for them to sit down. The man in charge wasted no time to start his spill. Without even a greeting, he stated forcefully. "We believe that the men who have your father are behind all these teleportation robberies. They have stolen a vast fortune. These robberies are so unique that the criminals are superheroes in the underworld. This is a disastrous combination. Thieves everywhere are willing to work for them. Informants will snitch telling them locations of great hidden treasures. Our whole world could fall apart as we know it. Do you understand how serious this is?" Before Amy and Zach could answer, he answered his own question. "No treasure anywhere is safe. Paranoia is sweeping the world! Everyone, everywhere is becoming terrified of teleportation thefts."

Red was pondering, "Why are they so concerned with the heat in the building? They beat me – they inflict serious hurt. Why compassion talk?" Gene asked, "Why did you go to Africa? You did not go to sit in a worship service in a strange language in sweltering heat. Why did you go?" "I was looking for answers." Gene sneered, "You thought you would find life's answers from the helpless. This story is getting really good. You were right, Ma, we do have to listen." "I went because their hearts beat so strongly! I wanted to experience the great joy in the midst of suffering." Ma and Gene swapped turns jeering, "Oh, my poor achy heart! Somebody, help me!" "I'm drowning in pain!" "Help me!" "Help me!" "Somebody help me!" "I can't take it anymore!" They turned to each other and laughed so hard. "You are so full of crap, old man!" "That was a good excuse." "It sounds plausible!"

Together they continued insults with every sound. "No one goes to the most helpless for help! If they could help themselves, they would not be so poor!" They paused, then continued in unison, "No! You were searching for the secrets of teleportation. Don't lie to us! We know the truth." They just couldn't resist mocking with a little more echoing off of each other. "My heart is breaking!" When one spoke, the other sniffled. "Somebody, help me!" "I'm all alone!" "Oh, hoh, hoh, hoh!" "I'm ruined!" "This is the worst thing ever!" The mockers turned and stared at each other frantically while trying to wipe all the imaginary tears off their faces.

All of a sudden, they grow serious and yelled, "Not!" They both jammed their faces right in front of Red's face. "You don't go to the most helpless for life's answers." "So why would he go?"

"I don't know! Oh, wait! I almost forgot. They are the keepers of teleportation!" "Oh, that makes sense!" "You sly dog!" "You pretended to need them to get them to reveal their great secret!" "What a genius of a plan!"

Officer Œil ranted, "I have figured this out. There is another way of looking at all this. Red may not be a victim at all. This whole kidnapping thing seems to have been staged. Your story is that you broke free from a giant of a man, outran with only one shoe a man who runs like a rabbit, your worst enemies saved your life, and in the massive shoot-out with bullets going everywhere, no one was hit? Are you kidding me or what? To make things even crazier, you would invite the whole school to witness what? It was all a pretense to make you a beloved victim and hero." He looked squarely at them, "Is all this beginning to make sense now? How else could Red be such an expert on teleportation without equipment? Of course, it was hidden! Staged!"

Ma accused, "You know more about teleportation than you are telling us!" Gene arrogantly declared, "A whole lot more, and you will tell us!" Ma continued, "Tell us, misery!" "Pain!" "Torment!" "Suffering!" "Real crying!" They both laughed at that one! "You can't imagine the pain coming your way!" "We are promising you two things. One, you will tell us! Two, tell us now and you will suffer a lot less." "Once we start torturing, we often have too much fun and continue long after we have learned all we need to know." "This teleportation secret will cost you everything; all you can choose is how much you will suffer." Red teared up with a sudden memory. He avoided blinking with his throbbing eyes from the beatings so that tears wouldn't escape and run down the cheek. Red remembered the words of the hotdog vendor, "The adventure will cost you everything!" The exact same words, "will cost you everything" were spoken as a warning about a future to come, and then had become a reality.

A man in a white coat entered the investigator's office, "I have created the teleportation inhibitor just as you asked for." The investigator asked the man to continue, "Explain to our guests what this handy-dandy gadget will do." "Teleportation is still science. Things can't disappear in one place and reappear in another. Things have to be changed in some sort of wave to travel long distances quickly without being seen. What this machine does is send out all sorts of radio, light waves, and other kinds that I will not discuss that will disrupt the teleportation flow giving all sorts of extra false readings that would destroy whatever or whoever is being teleported. The next time someone teleports into this light trap, most likely that person will be no more." In a great swagger, the officer declared, the next time you teleport, it will be the last thing you ever do … Oh, and one more thing, it has a little battery pack so that it will always stay on even if the electricity is cut." Amy and Zach just looked at each other dumbfounded.

The investigator commanded, "Both of you come here and see how it works." Both youngsters stayed seated out of great confusion and concern. "Well, c'mon! Are you hiding something that you do not wish for us to know? Come here." Amy and Zach rose and marched toward the gadget. The officer told the scientist, "Turn it on!" The inventor reached down and flipped on the switch. Immediately, the room was filled with light. Zach kept walking, but Amy stayed in the middle of the room. The two police were extra still. Zach spoke out, "Real funny! You two are acting like something weird happened. You can quit the act now; it is not funny!" Neither moved. He said, "Amy! Amy?" All of a sudden, he realized that she was not at his side. He returned and grabbed her hand to pull her to the middle. He then realized that she was frozen. He bounded back to the men and poked both men in the eyes. Neither blinked, nor flinched. Without thinking he flipped off the machine.

Just then Gus popped in the room, "I have the food!" His words were garbled since he was talking with a mouthful. Ma snapped, "You started eating without us! Where are your manners, boy!"

Gene ignored the interruption. Gene declared, "You will tell us right now how you obtained this teleportation chemical right now, or we will start breaking every bone in your body! Do you understand?" Red resigned himself to telling at least part of the story, "It all started with a hotdog vendor!" "Are you trying to tell me that there was a hotdog vendor back in the village? You're insane!" Red waits till he has a chance to continue, "The vendor had the strangest cart. The cart was painted with butterflies and …" Before Red had a chance to finish, Gus finished his sentence, "lightning!" Ma and Gene turned and stared at him. At the same time, they asked, "Did you see that cart in Africa?" "No!" "How did you know?" "He sold good hotdogs. You should eat yours." Ma asked, "You mean there is one of the same hotdog stands here?" Gus was confused, "I suppose it is the same. I have only seen the one here." She commanded, "Let's go see him." Red asked, "You mean you had to pay?"

The two law enforcers popped back in great surprise to see Zach standing right in front of them. All of a sudden, a huge grin assaulted the investigator, "I knew it! I knew it all along. You two are teleporters. You are bank robbers." In horror, Zach stepped back. Amy was dumbfounded, "How did you get way over there?" The officer declared, "Don't you play all innocent like, it won't help you any." Zach started walking backwards slowly. Mr. Thinks-he-knows-it-all screamed, "Turn that contraption back on, it was messing with his teleporting abilities." The lab jacket reached down and flipped the switch. Just like that, once again, everything stopped except for Zach. He ran over to his book. What he did not get was why as he was running past Amy, she kept flickering on and off. She started moving, froze, and started moving again. Time was in a terrible flux. As Zach ran, in his motion, at intervals, his fingers that had picked up the butterfly wing slipped out of the direct reach of the anti-teleporting light.

Zach surged forward. Amy turned around and stared at him. Finally, time resumed normal function. With her back to the men, they were shielded from seeing what Zach was doing. He opened the book, and saw only words. He flipped the page and still no treasure. He thumbed through the pages. He spotted one, but his time was running out. The one in charge instinctively did what he had done many times before. He raced ahead; and in a swift coordinated effort, he grabbed Zach's wrist and swooped out the cuffs. As the arm was being grabbed, Amy flipped her wrist and let her finger encounter the paper like wing. Upon contact, the butterfly's appendage unexplainably vanished.

Zach was spun down to the ground. The second set of clicks echoed through the air. Zach was now belly down, cuffed and a huge man was resting on him. Amy looked at her finger; she knew that somehow the wings-controlled teleportation. She raised her finger up in the air and turned it every way as if she was oblivious to Zach's great plight. Once the finger caught direct light from the anti-teleportation machine, the world stopped. She kept her index and thumb up. She walked over to the idle pair on the floor. She checked the visible shirt pocket with her other hand for keys – nothing! She slid her hand between the captor and prisoner and checked the other shirt pocket. She mumbled, "Nothing!" She patted the closest pants pocket. A faint, "clink" responded. She reached in, "This is just gross. It is freaking me out. Please! Please! Please! Don't let me touch his heirlooms."

She grabbed the metal; and with much zeal, she yanked the silver out. It is round all right, but not key round. There were so many coins that she could not see the bottom of the stack. Unknowingly, she let her upheld hand turn out of the light. In victory, he declared, "See, you teleport! I got you!" Immediately, she spun her hand back. All became quiet again. She twisted her hand full of change slowly. Layer by layer, the coins slid out until nothing was left. "No, no, no, no! I don't want to reach in that other pocket!"

Only a small corner of the pocket remained visible. She buried her fingers in the gap and felt nothing. The angle was all wrong to slide her hand in. She had to lay down on top of the man in order to angle her hand down the scary pit. "Yuck, yuck, yuck, yuck, yuck! No, no, no, no, no! Please, please, please, please, please!" She went silent then ripped her hand out of the dungeon of doom triumphantly. She raised her hand and waved the keys.

She drove the key toward Zach, but his hands were covered by the corpse like body on top of him. She tried to push her hand in, but it would not go. She slid around to Zach's other side. She attempted to force her hand in, but to no avail. She stood up, awkwardly, because one hand had to stay in the air. She snagged a fistful of shirt and yanked, but the cop barely moved. She stood and talked to herself, "What do I do? I can neither free Zach's hands to uncuff him nor remove this crazy man."

Very calmly, she walked over to the table. Picked up the light, and strolled back over to her restrained hero that was pinned on the ground. She laid down on the ground next to Zach and searched for his fingers under the man.

She angled the light between the two. Zach came to life. Immediately, he withdrew, his fingers buried deeper under the man. "No, no, no! Seriously Zach! You don't even know what is for your own good."

She tried to get the foot traction to drive her hand further within the human pile, but her feet just slipped. She attached her free hand to the man above to give herself pulling power. She yanked with the intention of freeing Zach's hand. The zombie began to tilt toward her. "Stop! Stop! Stop!" She released, and he receded back to his previous location. "I promised myself, I would never, ever touch a man's rear before marriage; and now, I am touching it, not just with one hand, but two." She slid the first half of her fingers between the belt portion of his pants and his body, and she used that leverage to slowly work the other hand. She located his fingers and thumb and pulled until his fingers were back in the light. Once again, he was turned back on. She yelled, "Don't move!"

He just stayed there for a moment trying to figure out the puzzling situation. He spoke, "Is that your hand on my derriere?" "Maybe!" "You wait till I blacked-out and then you take advantage of me." "Do you want me to leave you here?" "No!" "If you want out, kiss me." "Um, um!" "Just what I thought, you dated the three prettiest girls all at one time in math class, and you never kissed any of them. You are afraid to kiss me." "You are wrong!" "Are you trying to tell me you kissed a girl before?" "No, the three, they aren't the prettiest, there is one far prettier." Both glowed red. They could not hide their fanatical attraction nor their embarrassment. "And who would that be? Who is prettier than they?" "It is the girl who is holding the key to my heart and to my handcuffs! You have to help me out before I can kiss you." "He is too heavy for me. You have to get him off, but your fingers have to stay in the light." With ease, Zach rolls the uniform off as Amy held his hand still. She unlocked him. They both seized the anti-teleportation machine with their fingers dangling in the light. They stared at each other and floated in slowly for the kiss. Their lips touched and their eyes twinkled. He collected the book, and off they went.

As they arrived near the entrance, he yelled, "Wait!" She stopped hard, "What?" He leaned over and kissed her cheek. "Hurry up! We don't have all day!" She peered at him a little confused with the mixed commands, but she was warm all over. As they were exiting out the front door, he disappeared. She looked back at him. He had become just as lifeless as everyone else. She removed her fingers from the light. On cue, he resumed running, and everyone else was back to normal. She said, "C'mon! I know just the place." "Where are we headed?" "Are you hungry for a hotdog?" "Nothing could be better!"

CHAPTER 24
THE PARK

An old lady was creeping along. In one hand she held a cane, her other hand was clinging to a man beside her. Next to them was Red slumped in a wheelchair wearing a hoodie that was so big that it covered the face. A second attendant was pushing the rolling seat. They paused for a moment; and the one, who so gently guided the chair, pulled back the engulfing garment just above the eyes. "Is this the cart? Is this the one?"

The hotdog salesman never looked at the small group, but yelled out before the covered figure could answer, "Hello, Highly Esteemed One! You are dearly loved and have been sifted and tried by the Almighty. Hang in there, your sufferings will not last much longer. You have proven yourself willing to lose it all." The chair guide growled out, "I am the one who decides his fate, not you." Monkabe stared at Gene, "You went to Africa to control supernatural powers, but they will control you. Evil spirits take pleasure in letting you gloat for a little while before they terrorize you. Great fear is coming." Gus interrupted, "Maybe we should just be quiet so that he does not curse us anymore." Ma yelled at him, "Shut up you weak son. You are such a disgrace." Monkabe, "Go seal your doom; but remember, the grace of God is still calling out to whoever will listen." Just like that, the cart was gone.

Amy and Zach were racing up to the spot hand in hand. They encountered the location, but the cart had truly disappeared. Zach began then was interrupted, "It always has appeared that

God is nowhere to be found when needed most ..." With great speed Amy blurted out, "but that is where faith comes in!" "Hey, you stole my words, thief." Just then two gals stepped in between Amy and Zach! They halted in a stance where their bodies looked out of joint, then they went wagging, "No, no!" with their heads and their index fingers. They glanced at Amy, "Let us show you how it is done." "Look, and learn!"

The third girl put both of her hands on his chest and pushed him back slowly. Zach was very confused, but he was certain of one thing, their stunts would stay magnificent. His thinking skills at this moment had been greatly diminished to the point he was unaware of the obstacle behind him. He felt something at the knees. He started to turn his head to look at the item, but his sexy guide just shoved him. Zach rammed to a stop on a bench. She spun around slowly, raised her hands above her head, and tilted over backwards. "Catch me!" She cried as she fell. He reached out and scooped her. As she was being drawn in, she glanced back a mighty big smile at Amy who responded with very tight lips. The flirtatious one nestled up tightly resting her head on his shoulder. The other two ran up, one jumped on the bench, draped her body across the back of his shoulders and curled her head close to his.

The other one found her position, from a frontal position. She stepped on both of his feet, and let herself go forward. That one remaining exposed portion of his head became covered. They left him one eye to stare at a shell-shocked Amy. "This precious, dashing man is risking his life for you." "For what?" "Remember how this is done!" "You pucker the lips!" From all three, a lost in love sigh escaped and securely connected lips to face. One raised one hand as far out as possible and was holding a device that would forever capture the moment. Zach was having what would have been the moment of his life, and yet, his heart had already been given to Amy.

All three hopped up and faced Amy. "Now that is how it is done!" "That was thrilling!" "He is hot, really hot!" They just stopped. No one moved. No one said anything. "Well, why are you still standing there?" "Wasting time is not going to help any!" Amy was always so unsure of their games, not knowing all the twists until humiliation was total and then they always found the perfect little cruelty with which to serenade at the end. Amy was having great difficulty sizing this up. She knew they were protecting Zach as always, but were they doing it at her expense, or were they looking after her too – their way. Her thoughts were interrupted. "It's your turn!" "He is risking his life for you!" Amy still just stood there. Two flowed in behind her. With the outer hand, they each seized an arm to keep her from escaping. With the other in the back, they push her forward. Amy stepped up quickly two steps so that she could lean backwards and fight this super embarrassing moment.

The two quit pushing. "I guess she does not wish to kiss Zach." "What a shame!" "Such a loss!" "Maybe…" "Maybe what?" "You got to tell us!" "Maybe, just maybe, she does not know how to kiss him." "Surely, that is it!" "She has never kissed a man before!" "All she needs is another demonstration!" "Ah, that is right!" "Let's show her." "Do you think we can all kiss him on the lips at the same time?" "I am sure of it!" "When have we ever failed?" The two released Amy and walked past her. As soon as they passed her, they gave a bouncing joyful skip.

For the first time, Zach said something, and he picked a good time to support his dream girl. "C'mon, Amy!" He reached out his hands toward her. One girl slapped him. The other two grabbed him by the ear lobes and yanked him off his duff. "Where are your manners?" "Get up and honor her presence!" One girl pushed Amy forward, and the other two drug Zach closer by the ears. They lifted up the couple's arms and gingerly draped them around each other. "Much better!" "Mighty fine pose!" "But nothing! No kissing! Nothing!" "It's like a gun without bullets!"

The one whose car got riddled barked out, "Hey, you don't need to bring up guns and bullets."

Amy leaned in aiming straight for the lips. Her lips brushed off his and she planted a long slow kiss on his cheek. She backed up and rested her lips rested on his. Zach's eyes grew really big. She kissed tenderly; Zach reacted by returning the pucker. Right at the moment when he could claim to kiss back. She popped back and slapped him gently across the face. The audience reacted quickly. "Good use of the hand!" "Couldn't have done better myself!" "He deserved it for not standing to honor you."

All three gals lined-up to one side to give Amy a gigantic high five. Amy swung hard to meet the sailing hand. It stung, but she did not care. She swung again with all her might, and once more. For the first time, Amy felt like an equal honored member of the group, but the very next moment pushed her even beyond that. "Two hands!" "He deserved it!" Zach protested, "Hey-ey-ey!" "Now!" came the third." She flapped her wings in, in rhythm, with all her gusto. The first zipped behind Zach, locked back for a two-handed tomahawk swing. Amy responded. Over his shoulders and by his ears their hands squarely met! The extra loud sound startled Zach into a flinch. With great speed, the other two joined-in the double high five celebration over Zach.

Quickly, the three chameleons popped into a different mood. One clothed herself with his right arm, another nestled into the other arm, and the third stood really close in front and draped an arm around his neck. All three used one hand to hug; with the other, their fingers were walking all over his torso and face. "Zach, you know, we have always looked out for you above all others." "The other guys dreamed to be you." "You are the only guy who held our attention." Zach knew that this moment was probably not going to end as well as it started.

The gentleness vaporized into hostility. One grabbed his chest hairs, yanked, and held. Another grabbed a handful of hair and tugged his head back and to the side. The last one snatched the face centerpiece and churned the nose. Zach panted, "Ah, ah, ah, ah!" He received severe warnings. "Don't forget to treat her with great honor." "You had better treat her with the same honor we treated you!" "Or we will be back, and you won't like it!"

The three turned to Amy and gave a slight bow. "He is all yours now!" "Follow our example!" "We give you all rights to him!" Zach protested, "Hey, I am not a thing to be owned!" Just like that, without another word, they sprinted off.

Zach exclaimed, "We came to the park to find Monkabe so that we could understand God's plan, and not to be distracted by the gals." "I think God spoke quite clearly." "We are no closer to solving things." "Oh, are we? You went from being the escort of the three most popular girls at the same time to being my possession. God spoke loudly and clearly!" Zach faded a great sigh, "OHHhhh!"

"Are you questioning what God said?" "Ouch!"

The traffic had stalled Sabrina on the blacktop, "A traffic jam at this time of the day is rare ... Look, police are roaming the park!" Mickey exclaimed, "Let's go see." "It is probably not safe." "You are right! It is probably not safe for Red and his family." "There is nothing we can do." "If we don't look and see, we will always regret it!" Sabrina pulled in to an empty parking spot. "Thank you, Momma!"

Zach was thumbing through the book. "There are only two butterfly wings left!" "That means, we can each teleport once more." Amy suggested, "Let's look at the butterflies. Maybe they will give us a clue!" "They are totally black," "and then there is the brightest yellow." An idea was forming in their heads. "Totally pitch dark black – the kind of dark where you can't even see your hand in front of your face as you bring it closer until it hits your nose." "Bright yellow – just like on the cart – the yellow lightning." "You got to be kidding me!" The main yellow on the wings!" "Crazy, isn't it?" "Is shaped like lightning." "God is the light in the darkest day." "And He comes with power!"

The three girls reached the edge of the park, "Oh, no!" "Oh, no what?" "I see it – police!" "They are here for Zach and Amy!" "It is bad enough that the teleporting gang is hunting down Amy!" "Now the police are, too!" "They need our help!" "We have helped lots!" "You got shot at!" "We gave money to them!" "We banded together the school to chase away the shooters." "We gift tied Zach as a gift to Amy!" "That was a good one!" "This is different! If we help and get caught, the police will think that we are a part of the teleporting bandits." "Being wanted by the police would ruin our reputation!" "And our lives!" "So, what do we do?"

Zach continued, "The main yellow is lightning, but many more yellow splotches are along the edge. What do they mean?" "Not every part has to have meaning." "But it does have to have meaning if it is a miraculous butterfly!" Amy asked, "So what do the yellow splotches have to do with the story?" Zach emits a stuttered, "Oh, oh!" "What?" "I can't tell you!" "How come you can't tell me? We are being hunted by the good guys and the bad guys. You have an idea and you won't share it. I'm hurt!" "I can't!" "Please!" "I just can't! It is not appropriate." "You have got to tell me!" "Don't laugh at me or tease me! Do you promise?" "Okay, I promise!" "They look like yellow gold rings!" "You are thinking this is a sign that we will get married?" "I told you. It is just a thought." "Well, get that thought right out of your head. You and me getting married." "Please!" Amy reached up and caresses both sides of his face with her hands. She pulled him slightly forward and kissed him on the lips! Let that thought go for a moment or two but not for very long."

Sabrina declared, "There is Amy and some guy! ... Take that back – and a boyfriend." "I'll distract the police!" "I will warn Amy!" Mickey started to leave. Sabrina turned and asked, "What are you going to do to distract the police?" "You don't want to know, Mom. Just go, it will be alright! I promise!" "I'm trusting you."

"Tell me, so what do the splotches have to do with things, since my idea was wrong?" "No, not wrong, just an added bonus!" "They are alternating side by side in a line." Amy and Zach turn and slowly started walking down the sidewalk. They were both looking so intently into the book that a mishap happened. Zach stepped on Amy's foot. "Hey, you stepped on my foot!" "You put your foot under mine!" She shoves him. Zach declares, "They look like footsteps." "You are right! It is just like Scripture, 'Uphold my steps in Your paths, that my footsteps may not slip,' Psalms 17:5" "That is amazing! Not only does God ordain where the steps go, but He holds each step so that the foot will not slip." "You will like the verse that goes before it, too." "Well, what is it?" "Concerning the works of men, by the word of Your lips, I have kept away from the paths of the destroyer." You are right, I do! Everything is pitch black dark around us, but He lights our footsteps and holds our steps if we listen …" He paused so that she could join him. Together, "to what He says."

Sabrina walked on by without looking at Zach or Amy. In a nonchalant voice she said, "The police are surrounding the park." Zach looked up and whispered, "Who's that!" "Sabrina?" Zach looked all around; he could see the police working their way closer. "We are in big trouble." "Keep your eyes off trouble, and pay full attention to the words from His mouth." "You are right. These are our steps, but the footprints have already been set. He holds, we listen!" "That is the truth, but we can't see the footprints glow even before we step – we just have to believe they are."

Mickey was climbing a tree, getting higher and higher. He stopped, located the wanted and then climbed higher. "I hope this works!"

Sabrina continued to walk in the same direction. She knew if she returned back to Mickey, she would order him to stop. She just couldn't bear to look. She spotted people in costumes. It was strange to see people in costumes at this time of the year.

As she drew closer, she heard their intense questioning. "Where did they go?" "I don't know!" "We got to find them." Once again, Sabrina continued to walk without looking, "In the big bushes up ahead on the right!"

The three turned and looked at each other. All of a sudden, one reached behind and slapped the back of another, "You're it!" The other two took off running. After a long sprint, one stopped at a tree, "This is base, I'm safe!" "No bases!" "Yes, way!" "There has to be bases." The 'it' walked closer and closer. Finally, it tagged. "You're it! No bases." The it, who was no longer it, ran in a totally different direction. The other girl joined the escape. The one at the tree waited a moment then sprinted off after them. As they went, they squealed in delight. They ran into the bushes and stopped. There standing in front of Amy and Zach were characters in a costume of a lion, a chicken, and a monkey.

Sabrina not could stand it any longer. She knew that her son was going to do something really frightening. She had made her way back to him. She spotted him high in a tree and whispered, "Whatever you are planning, don't do it!"

The three costumes were walking down the sidewalk. The police stopped them. "I need to see your faces before you can proceed out." one official blared. Way off to the side were two young women, and one of them had earbuds in. The lion asked the police, "What is going on?" The police ignored the question, she plodded on, "You are on a manhunt, aren't you?" She turned to the monkey, "This is so exciting; I can't wait to tell everyone!" Amy had never played the girls' game. She had been played by the games, but not played. She went along, "Everyone is going to be jealous of us for missing out in all the excitement. The police turned to the third and said, "Can we see your face, please?" The lion leaned into the chicken, and where no one could see, she slid her hand up the backside of the head gear.

The two girls off to the side were playing their game even when they did not seem like they were in it. The one with the headset commanded in a soft voice, "Act like a chicken!" The chicken locked the arms in the armpit and flapped the arms stiffly. The lion slumped a little like it was lurking. With the free hand she clawed at the air. From the lion comes a "GRRR!" Amy scratches her sides to mimic a monkey. From behind, the lion turns her hand inside the face gear of the chicken with a cellphone. A female voice came from the chicken, "Bawk, bawk, bawk!"

The police obviously heard three female voices coming from the different costumed characters. Like always, there was so much distraction, that the police had a hard time sorting things out.

In the tree, a little distance away, a young lad, who had been laying on a large branch had also been looking on waiting for just the right moment. He muttered to himself, "Showtime!" He hooked the back of his jeans on a notch sticking out, then he let go of the tree and fell. There dangling by the back of his pants, real fear took over and he let it rip, "Ahhh! Ahhh! Ahhh!" Everyone turned and stared; way up in a tree a young boy's life being saved by twig.

Mickey was right, his mother would not have wanted to know his plan. She could not help herself, "Somebody help my baby! Somebody, help my baby." Mickey felt himself slipping. He looked over and the three costumes were still there in front of the police.

The lion announced, "Let's go take a look!" The other two took a step in that direction. The policeman orders, "No, you three need to go home! This park is not yet secured. They walked past the police having bluffed their way through with a little help.

A couple of policemen ran up. One immediately gave orders, "Son, look at me! Look at me!" He looked away and he could not tell if the costumes had been released from the park. He stared and all he could see was a tree blocking his view. He looked at the policeman, "Can you reach the branch right above your head?" Mickey felt he needed to buy more time. He yelled, "Somebody help me! Somebody help me!" Sabrina realized for the first time in her life she needed to be hysterical in a crisis moment. "My baby! My baby! My baby! Don't fall! Oh, my goodness, don't fall! The policemen were trying to regain control of the situation. One stood directly on front of Sabrina, "Ma'am! Look at me! You are not helping the situation! You need to be calm for your son!" The other in a bossy tone, "You need to quit moving! You are going to make yourself fall! Look at me! Calm down! Everything will be all right!"

Mickey peeked out to the edge of the park. He saw the characters leaving unescorted by police. Mickey wondered, "How can I signal mom that they are gone without tipping everyone off?" Mickey waved his hands as if out of fear; he also gave his head the smallest of nods. The policeman, who was focused on the mom, said, "Calm down! You don't want to make your son panic any more than he is!" She looked at the officer squarely! "You're right! She slowed the waving of her arms. She had to know exactly what that nod meant. Was it saying they are gone, so she asked, "Are you alright, son?" "Yes, I'm fine! Everything is fine!" "Good calm down, and the policeman will tell you what to do." The policeman questioned once again, "Can you grab that branch just above your head? He reached out and grabbed. Without waiting anymore, Mickey wiggled his pants free. The policeman declared, "Just stay right there and we will have someone to get you down in a moment." Mickey did not want to be questioned. He climbed downwards. At one spot, his foot slipped and his body launched downwards. While the feet slipped away, his hands held fast. His feet were now dangling over nothing. He chose to swing back and forth ever creating a wider pendulum until his foot reached. Moments later, he was on the ground safely.

The officers continued to take command of the situation. One spoke to her, "Ma'am, calming down saved your son's life. Your son responded to your change in attitude, and he started thinking." The other, "You cannot climb trees in the park. You need to wait just a minute and a paramedic will check you out." Mickey responded, "I'm fine! I want to leave! I don't like everyone staring at me!"

With that Sabrina wrapped her arm around her son's neck and pulled him in close. She whispered, "You scared me to death! I thought you were going to fall. Don't ever do that again… I am so proud of you." She turned in such a way where no one else could see his face. He just smiled. Sabrina reached out, grabbed his nose, and yanked. "Ow, what was that for?" "For pretending to slip at the end!" He smiled again.

CHAPTER 25
THE PLAN?

A gray-haired lady was pushing a slumped over man with thick dark glasses in a wheel chair. They entered a small downtown diner. She just talked to him the whole time knowing he was not going to answer. There was a little bump up as they entered the door. The lip was not too big for the wheelchair to bounce over it. "Ah, there we go – we made it. This place is beautiful. The jukebox looks like it came from the sixties. You remember how we used to sing to the music. I always tried to get you to go dancing with, but you were just too shy. The floor is the old black and white alternating squares. This is the kind of place you always liked. You remember we would go out every Friday night and get a milkshake. Today is a perfect day to grab another shake. I will get you strawberry, your favorite." The whole time, he was slumped over in his ride not responding to a thing.

They found a small table in the corner. A man hopped up from his booth and kindly pulled a chair away so that she could scoot her man up to the table. She turned and smiled, "Thank you so much! You are such a kind man!" "No, problem! Is there anything else I could do for you?" "That is all we need for now. Your kindness makes the day so much richer." "Yes, Ma'am!" He turned and walked away.

A lady delivered two shakes. "Here you go: one chocolate and a strawberry shake. Is there anything else I can get for you?" "No … Yes, there is, he drools a lot. Can I have a couple of extra napkins?" Shortly after, the waitress returned with a huge wad of napkins. "Oh, that is more than plenty. You are so thoughtful. Thank-you!"

She picked-up his shake with one hand; and with the other, she guided the straw into his mouth. "Okay now, you can drink from the straw. You must suck hard because the shake is a little thick … Keep sucking! There you go!" He began to cough. She saw the shake escaping from the corner of his mouth. She quickly grabbed a couple of napkins and caught the excretions before they rolled off the face. "Would you like me to read to you? Would you like to help me hold the book?" She reached down and held his hand and lifted it up gently. She slipped the book into his fingers and held his hand securely on the book.

She leaned over ever so closely, and whispered, "Anything else I can do for you?" "That about me drooling was a bit much don't you think?" "You didn't really have to drool!" "I had to act the part and make you clean my face." "Anything for you, dear!" She pulled the book up closer. "Look at those wings! They have to tell us more about how to solve this riddle." "So, what do we know so far?" "The splotched look like footsteps where he lights our paths and firmly holds our steps." "I figured out why lightning bolts are a part of the story." "Why is that?" John 8:12 says, "Then Jesus spoke to them again, saying, "I am the light of the world. The one who follows Me shall not walk in darkness, but shall have the light of life." God is the light of the world and He lights our path! The brightest naturally occurring light in this world is the lightning bolt.

Amy quoted Revelations 4:11, "You are worthy, O Lord, to receive glory, and honor, and power; for You created all things, and by Your will they came to be and were created." "The lightning bolt – the great symbol of light and power! All things exist by His power and for His glory. Can you feel His glory?" "No, I don't feel His power or His glory." "Neither do I!" "How about this one in Colossians 2:10, 'and you are complete in Him, who is the head of all rulers and power.' Do you feel complete right now because of His power?" "Sometimes, when I don't care and content trusting, I feel his supernatural power. When I am concerned how things end, I feel miserable. Do you?" "At this moment, yes I feel his incredible peace because I am trusting Him to complete His plan." "We are hunted by the good-guys, and the bad-guys. We are powerless to help ourselves. We have no place to stay, and we can't hide for much longer." Together, "The time is perfect for His miracle!"

"So, we figured out the butterfly!" "Well, not exactly, there at the top of the wings are countless tiny dots. What do they mean?" "I didn't see those! They are innumerable like the stars in the sky except all jammed together." "There's more?" "There needs to be more! We need to understand the power and the victory!" "You're right!" "There are so many dots of lights that they look like a cloud." "You said, "Cloud?" "Oh, that is right! Hebrews 12" Together they quoted, "Since we are surrounded by such a great a cloud of witnesses, let us lay aside every burden, and the sin which so easily entraps *us,* and let us run with perseverance the race that is set before us," "The cloud of witnesses are" "the saints that have gone before us." "They testify that God is all power," "the Light of the World," "He lights and upholds our steps," "This is for His great pleasure," "and all power has been given us!" "For what? Let's continue saying the passage." Together, "looking to Jesus, the author and perfector of *our* faith, who for the joy that was set before Him bore the cross, and scorning the shame. Sat down at the right hand of the throne of God." "Christ won because He paid for my rebellion with His life at the cross!" "We get to join Him forever because He forgave us!"

Amy whispered, "This is too good to be true." "What is that?" "You see the red dots on both sides?" "No way. The story is not complete without the blood of the cross."

"If Christ went to the cross, and paid the price giving us eternal life, why do we have to go to our own crosses like running for our lives?" "You have to be kidding me? There is still more to this story!" "You are right! The missionary loved the butterfly story. He would often tell those butterflies started off as ugly, gross ..." "caterpillars. They would cocoon and appear dead!" "They would break out of the web coffin as butterflies." "They went from being all slow and ugly" "to being the flying flowers of the animal kingdom." "They were transformed from being the worst to being the most beautiful of animals."

"The winning comes with a big price." "Are you ready?" "Ready!" One last time, they whisper together, "To the cross! To our transformation!"

The edge of the perimeter was lined with reporters. In fact, a huge crowd had assembled to see if the great heist would take place. The phenomenon of teleportation had attracted people from all over the world. Amy was pushing Zach in the wheelchair. They arrived about 50 yards from the barricade set up by the police, but could go no further because of the multitude. Amy turned Zach so he could watch the reporters not far away. "Is teleporting real or is it a hoax? One of the greatest collections of treasures is arriving in a few minutes. Priceless artifacts from all over the world will be on display here. The police have assured that needed precautionary measures have been taken so that the teleportation ring cannot take the wonders that belong to the world. The prime time to steal will be when the pieces arrive before they are securely vaulted."

Amy leaned over Zach, "Do you have any ideas?" "Not a clue!" "So, what do we do?" "I wish I knew!" "Even if we were able to sneak-in, how do we catch some vicious criminals?" "Our plan is perfect except for the details." "Let's do it, then!"

CHAPTER 26
MONKABE

Seemingly out of nowhere, a swarm of men seized Zach and Amy with one man double clutching each arm. A fifth man stood behind them talking on the radio, "Suspects are now in custody!" The plainclothesmen were squeezing hard. Amy yelped, "Ow, ow! No need to grab us. If we wanted to teleport out, we would and there is nothing you could do about it." Zach chimed in, "We did not come to steal, but to stop the thefts from happening." The five officers looked at each other confused and startled for they were so proud of themselves for having caught mastermind criminals. They eased their grip a little, but still fastened on firmly.

The two were brought to the command center. Arrogantly, officer Œil belittled, "So you have come to be heroes and stop the thefts from happening." Amy and Zach said nothing. "So, what can be done to stop the thefts?" Amy responded, "Nothing that we know of; but especially, don't use your lights." "So, you think you two can come in here and talk us out of using our anti-teleportation device so that everyone else can steal. How dumb do you think I am?" The man in charge's shoulders were tucked way back, and his chest was swollen. With a quick snap, his head popped backwards.

Amy leaned over to Zach and whispered, "Why do all men strut like that? All he needs is a comb dangling from his head, and he would look exactly like a rooster with the same bounce." "What did I do to get thrown under the bus with men like him?" "Okay not you, but you did strut confidence. Do you remember the first time you came to my house? You brought one set of tools for one repair. I don't know how you were so lucky as to guess exactly what was wrong with my mower, but you amazed me. You have been good at that ever since."

"Will you two stop yakking? Let me tell you what is going to happen. You see, we have the lights that messed up your teleporting placed inside and outside the building. As soon as the delivery arrives, we will flood the place with extreme lights. We will disrupt the ability to control teleporting, and apprehend your crew. There is nothing you can do about it. I dare you to teleport out. As soon as you do, I will flood this place with lights. You and your crew will not be able to escape."

Zach turned to the gal who revs his motor. In low tones, he continued the teasing. "I can't believe you compared me to him." Zach nodded in the inspector's way. "You are no way like him. You are magnificent." The policemen guarding the two tried to hold it in, but a snicker popped out anyway. The one being referenced became defensive, "What are you snickering about?" Neither the policeman nor the two in love dared to answer.

You see this clicker right here? This is what controls the lights," gloated the one in charge. There is nothing you can do. See, I am in charge and I will take you and your crew down." Zach opened his mouth and said something he shouldn't have, "What keeps me from teleporting that clicker into my hand and teleporting out?" The gloating melted leaving the gloater speechless. "In fact, with teleporting powers, we are in total command if we want to be." Amy tried to calm the one she had chosen to be beside, "Zach, Zach!" "We can do anything we want to any of you!" A vicious tone erupted out of the leader, "Are you threatening us?" Amy blurted, "No, we are here on your side! I wish you could see that!" She reminded the man next to her, "You remember we have come to give our lives away, not fight for them." A look of sorrow contorted his face. He turned to their pompous captor, "I apologize for my outburst. I did not mean to disrespect you. Sorry!"

A crackle ripped out of the walkie-talkie, "We are arriving on schedule. Requesting permission to dock." The chief responded, "Permission granted. You may proceed."

One of the minor streets very close by was lined with media trucks and vans. Each one was highly decorated declaring their news brand. One extra small vehicle was moving very slowly. It, too, was decorated, but its brand was far less obvious except to the few who recognized it. This slow cruiser had yellow stripes; but they were not pin stripes, they were lightning strikes. Weaving around the bolts were butterflies. The peddler pushing it declared, "It's time my friends! It's time to do what you do!"

The chief declared, "I am going to supervise the unloading and catch me some burglars. You two will stay right here and miss all the excitement." The chief and two more left. Zach and Amy were still surrounded by the same five who captured them in the first place.

The ventriloquist box spoke without moving at all, "Opening the doors... Entering... Inspecting package... Everything is as it should be... Turning on lights in three, two..." As soon as the word, "turning" resonated, Amy and Zach swiveled their heads to stare into each other's eyes. They nodded! As inconspicuously as possible, they each slid a thumb into their own waistline. Strapped securely, yet hidden was a small envelope. The thumb invaded the small paper container touching the butterfly wing. Very quickly they retrieved their thumbs. An overpowering weird light radiated from many sources. Everyone grew still except for the young pair.

"What do we do?" "I don't know! Let's go see what we can do!" They exited the command center and hurried toward the heavily guarded delivery truck. They watched Gene, Ma and Gus enter into the carriage with tank-like walls. The observers whispered at the same time, "Let's shut them in by closing those doors!" They sprinted in unison. As they approached the doors, with elbows out, they placed their hands right in front of their shoulders with palms forward to maximize a great shove.

What they had not noticed was the two frozen figures they just ran by. One was really tall and super wide, and the other was short and wiry. Frozen figures stay frozen when time stands still. Sometimes, active figures play possum faking as inactive, but simply in idle and quite aware.

Just as the sprinting couple passed, the two pretend-like mummies lunged out with each grabbing an arm and back of the collar. With a great yank, both were flipped over backwards and slammed on the ground. Zach attempted to reach out to his assailant. The giant holding him lifted him up slightly and slammed his prey down hard. "Give me an excuse to really hurt you!" Zach realized that he was overpowered and stopped. Amy was on the ground face down as well. She was lashing out trying to hit anything she could. The man holding her just laughed at her. "Is that the best you've got? That is pretty pitiful. You want to play?" He palmed the back of her head and started rocking her brain container back and both rubbing off the skin on the tip of her nose with the pavement.

Monkabe opened his cart, and retrieved a glass jar. He lifted it up high. He majestically flipped his wrist; unscrewing the lid; and sprung open the seal to the jar. "It is time my friends. Go and do what you do." One after another black butterflies with yellow lightning stripes floated out and flew. They were all headed in one direction as if on a mission.

The people snatchers twisted their victims' arms hard enough that the victims choose not to react hoping their arms wouldn't rip up. In one fluid motion, the contorted were yanked to their feet and were driven inside the truck. The big one boasted, "You are right Gene! Catching them was so easy because they would come running to us."

As they entered into the semi-trailer, they noticed a couple of large cases. Beyond wooden frames in the corner was Red and appearing quite worn from all the beatings. Ma commanded, "Shove them to the back of the trailer and let them go!"

As they were being released, Amy ran up to her dad and hugged him, "Oh, what have they done to you?" "I have never been better in my life!" "Oh, Daddy! You have always been amazing!" Zach strolled up slowly and halted. He was very unsure of his place in the family. The father asked, "Have you taken care of my daughter?" "Yes, sir!" The older man lifted up an arm to make room for a third person in the hug. Zach confessed, "Red, I am sorry I got your daughter caught." "You are right where you need to be!" "Thank you, Red!"

Ma asked, and all the others had questions as well. "Why do they call you, Red?" "When you had hair, were you a red-head?" "Did you burn easily in the sun?" "Where you hot-tempered and always glowing Red?" Red responded, "None of those! I was a blond and my name is Jared which was shortened to Red."

Ma boasted, "If you try to escape past us, we will just beat you." Gene snapped, "Ma, you mean 'we' as the rest of us; your beating would be totally useless." "Hush, son, respect your ma in her moment of glory!" Gene bowed sarcastically, "Sorry, Ma!" She continued, "In about five minutes you will freeze like the rest of the people. We have one more drop each left in the bottle, we will leave. You will be stuck here having teleported in and you cannot teleport out. What a crying shame!" Gene cackled, "Everyone will think you are the thieves." Ma turned to each one of her crew and offered them a drop. When it came her time, no more came out. She shook it down some more. She squeezed again and a little more slurped out.

In the glistening of the sunlight, the animal flowers gracefully floated in. The detained saw the butterflies and knew that God in His time speaks. Rather than landing on the captors to give them more time, they flew into the crates through knotholes.

Inside the crates were not hidden treasures, but frozen police officers. On each one, a butterfly landed, but the problem still remained. While alive the butterflies were ordinary. Only after death would they give away the power of conquering time. The officers did not flinch, twitch, or blink for they were fully dormant. The butterflies finished their mission. Each without cause just died to give away life.

Those transformed creatures from caterpillars followed the example set two thousand years ago, when on the cross, Jesus was nailed to die. God had come to die on the cross. Our Maker's fury over rebellion demanded death, so Jesus stretched out on the cross voluntarily. Before the crucifixion had finished its work, Jesus freely gave up His life and died. So, in the giving of His life, all can live who chose the God-payment for their revolt against the will of the Eternal One.

Red spoke, "I give you this – you pulled off some amazing heists." They all gloated, "All those teleportation robberies, we did them!" "We are so rich now!" "We don't need to steal anymore. We can become upstanding citizens of the community and be honored for our greatness."

Amy snapped back, "You can't leave us here to take the rap for your crimes!" In their unmeasurable arrogance, they blurted out more. "Red, you nearly denied us teleportation powers. You almost succeeded! In a way you did, teleporting powers have run out." Gene declared, "Everyone calls me genius because I am the mastermind of our escapades, but you are the smartest opponent I ever had. You are truly the genius. I give you that."

The two muscles who joined the group late spoke, "We have never been humiliated and outdone by a bunch of little girls especially you Amy." "Yeah, the way you got away from us is the most humiliating experience of our lives."

Zach asked, "You have said all sorts of great things about them two, what about me? Don't you have anything to say about me?" "Who are you and what have you done?" "Ouch, that hurts!" "Except we don't understand at all how you figured out to teleport as well. We are dumbfounded on that one!"

Ma wrapped it up, "None of that really matters, soon your teleportation session will end, and you will be stuck here." They all laughed. "What losers!" Gene squirmed in delight, "No one will come and teleport you out of prison. There is only one last teleportation jump left and the five of us will teleport out. You cannot save yourself by teleportation." Ma joined in, "Teleportation is over forever and you lose!"

Red bravely spoke up, "This is your last chance to surrender and end this honorably!" "Who are you to tell us what to do?" "You had been warned that fear was going to seize you. Your time has come to an end!" "You are serious, aren't you?" Red looked directly at Gus who had been silent the whole time, "Gus, you have followed your mom and brother all these years because you felt trapped. Now, as in right now, you must choose where you stand." Gene turned to his brother, "He is trying to divide us. It is the only hope he has. Don't listen to him." Gus finally spoke up, "I have hated what I have let you turn me into. I am so sorry for what I have done!" Ma snarled, "You are the worst son there ever was. We protected you from yourself. We have made you rich, and you reject us. You are absolutely despicable!"

Red continued, "You were warned that more you try to control the spirits, more that they would control you. Your time is done! Your lives as you have known it are now over. You will now experience the terror of being owned by what terrifies you most."

All of a sudden, the crates swung apart. Officer Œil and the team surrounded the bandits. The confusion radically became overwhelming as they all screamed but not in unison, "On your knees!" "Hands behind your head." Very quickly the crooks were handcuffed and rendered useless.

Officer Œil walked over to Zach and Amy and admitted, "I have never been so wrong about anyone in my life. I nearly ruined your lives; I should not have been so proud of my detective skills. I created things that were not there. You are very brave and honorable people." Amy gleamed a smile, "Thank you for admitting that. It took a lot of courage!" Zach continued, "In the end, you did save our lives."

Amy whispered in Zach's ear, "We and dad are about to freeze as well as everyone outside of this truck. The officers are about to see time stand still. They will hold us in some deep bunker until we tell them what we cannot explain." "I know!"

Zach turned to once so proud officer, "I would like a small gesture of belief in us from you?" "What's that?" "We know you truly believe us if..." Amy joins in, "you turn off your lights!" "But that is what kept you from teleporting?" With a sad puppy-dog face she questioned, "So, you really don't trust us after all!?" Zach informed, "The teleportation window is now closed. Accept it! Please!" The officer reached into his pocket and unveiled his clicker. "Everything within me screams to do what I believe is best, but it is the heart things like trust that make life worth living."

The staller had procrastinated too long, Amy and Zach took each other's hand. They interlocked fingers. They swung their hands backwards and forwards. Two thirds of the way through a swing, they froze. The stop was instantaneous faster than humanly possible. The Officer stares at them unbelievingly. In a subconscious effort to get things back to normal, he snaped the button. Even more stunning were the two love birds' ability to continue their motion back at the previous speed without any jerking or twitching of muscles. The one in blue declared, "You freaked me out for a moment. Your arms stopped in mid-swing. The life from you two was gone. As soon as I clicked this button you resumed as if you never stopped. How did you do that?" Zach poked a little at him, "Your imagination is really good – like thinking we were the masterminds of the greatest robberies in history." Amy just couldn't wait to make things a little more unnerving, "Maybe you were witnessing the beginning of catastrophic cosmic collapse by teleporting, and turning off those lights saved the universe." "Maybe you discovered the secret of teleportation." "You caught the teleportation bug." Amy and Zach marched on by just about unable to control a hysterical laughter fit. The great Officer Œil was lost staring into space.

Police cars with lights had littered the whole area. Officer Œil gloated to Ma and Gene. "You thought you were really something. Now they will lock you away where you will never be seen again. Every person you meet, you will fear. The interrogators will break you until you tell them how to teleport. Every guard will attempt to bribe you and threaten you to reveal your secret. The greed in all will eat you alive. Once you tell, your life will tragically end so that you won't repeat your secret ever again. Have a marvelous rest of your life!" Ma retorted, "But, we don't know how teleporting works. It just does!" Gene added in, "You heard us, we can't ever duplicate teleporting ever again." The officer gave parting words, "Good luck with the fear and torture, then! I can't stop it even if I wanted to."

Ma ripped her son apart, "I told you that framing Red for everything in the middle of the police trap was a terrible idea!" "Why are you griping at me? You always whine like a little baby when you are supposed to be the wise leader of the family. You belly ache even when you loved an idea just because you are a snot rag." "You called me a snot rag?!" The detective was fully amused and moved on.

Monkabe confronted Ma and Gene, "Evil spirits are seeking to torture your souls not only because you visited their hidden site, but also requiring payment for using supernatural powers for your own selfish gain. A petrifying abundance of fear is ready to pounce, and how long do you think God will be merciful and hold them back?" Ma and Gene shamefully stared downwards. "God is knocking at the door of your hearts. The All Merciful's arms are still open wide in eager anticipation. Run to Him while you still can!"

Officer Œil made his way over to big and little, "You, two, are going to prison." Now the gloating officer spewed an eerie chuckle, "You were beaten by weak, little girls. Where you are going, they will say things to each other with you standing there, 'Now, how many 4? 27?' 'Uhm hum! That's right. Four little girls beat you 27 different times.' They will all belittle you. Then they will hurt you and promise you this, 'Every time they see you, they will give you more pain. How many times a day do you think they will see you? 4? 27? No, 427 times a day!'" With that, he cranked out an evil roar.

Once again, Monkabe appeared, "He is not the one who decides your future." The officer's chest puffed out just a little bit more which seemed a little impossible considering how far it was puffed out before. The two criminals were flabbergasted. The cocky man in charge stuffed his thumbs inside the front edge of his belt to the sides of where his six-pack should be. Monkabe continued while pointing backward with his thumb. "Don't worry about him. He can't hear me or see me." Both men gulped. Their heads popped backward and then way forwards. The officer slid off to his next victim. Monkabe continued, "Why do you think it is so strange talking to an angel? You have spent all this time messing with supernatural powers. You tried to dirty His powers. The One who made you and gave you life. He who gave you so much talent that you have used to destroy. He is calling you. Are you tired of fighting Him yet? Listen to what He has to say." They both nodded. "The big miracle here is not that an angel is talking to you, but that the God of the universe wants you as much as ever even after all you have done. I am leaving now because the One who loves you most is knocking hard on your heart. Listen! Be amazed and let Him set you free on the inside and run with Him!"

[Author's note. The first and the last – The first thought of writing this book occurred about fifteen years earlier with the concept of lightning butterflies that stop time. The last piece of the puzzle came in 2019 when I went back to Africa to take a picture of a butterfly for the story. I only saw one butterfly while there – the one tailor-made for this story designed from the beginning of creation. God is unbelievably amazing.]

Made in the USA
Columbia, SC
16 November 2022